P9-EDO-938

BEWARE!!
DO NOT READ THIS
BOOK FROM
BEGINNING TO END!

It's bad enough that your mom thinks you still need a baby-sitter. Then Zoe from the KidsCare Agency turns up at your door. Whoa! Zoe has a rat tattooed on her ear. You have a feeling *bad* just got *worse*.

Zoe offers you a choice: fun? Or games? Whatever you choose, prepare for a scare! Can you take the horrors of the Fun Zone? Escape the Bottomless Ball Pit? Survive the swirling Sand Blob? Beat the evil games-master Dare at his own games?

This scary adventure is all about you. You decide what will happen. And you decide how terrifying the scares will be!

Start on PAGE 1. Then follow the instructions at the bottom of each page. You make the choices.

If you choose well, you may survive your baby-sitter nightmare. But if you make the wrong choice . . . BEWARE!

SO TAKE A DEEP BREATH. CROSS YOUR FINGERS. AND TURN TO PAGE 1 TO *GIVE YOURSELF GOOSEBUMPS*!

READER BEWARE —
YOU CHOOSE THE SCARE!

Look for more
GIVE YOURSELF GOOSEBUMPS adventures
from R.L. STINE

R.L. STINE

GIVE YOURSELF

Goosebumps®

ATTACK OF THE
BEASTLY BABY-SITTER

AN
APPLE
PAPERBACK

SCHOLASTIC INC.
New York Toronto London Auckland Sydney

A PARACHUTE PRESS BOOK

No part of this publication may be reproduced in whole or in part, or stored in a retrieval system, or transmitted in any form or by any means, electronic, mechanical, photocopying, recording, or otherwise, without written permission of the publisher. For information regarding permission, write to Scholastic Inc., 555 Broadway, New York, NY 10012.

ISBN 0-590-93485-6

12 11 10 9 8 7 6 5 4 3 2 1   7 8 9/9 0 1 2/0

Printed in the U.S.A.   40

First Scholastic printing, June 1997

DING DONG!

"Get the door, please!" your mom calls from upstairs. "It's the baby-sitter from Fun and Games KidsCare."

"I'm too old for a baby-sitter!" you yell for the hundredth time. "Stinko's the one who needs a baby-sitter. Or maybe a zookeeper would be better!"

"Mom!" your six-year-old brother whines. "I'm not a Stinko!"

"Stop calling your brother that silly name," your mother scolds as she hurries down the stairs. "I don't have time for arguments. Dad is waiting for me in the car." She smoothes her hair. "Now, answer the door and be nice. I don't want you torturing this baby-sitter like you did the last one."

"Who, me?" you ask innocently.

Your mother rolls her eyes.

DING DONG! DING DONG!

"I'm coming. I'm coming." You shuffle to the door and throw it open.

And come face-to-face with a giant pink bubble.

Turn to PAGE 2.

POP! The huge bubble bursts in the face of a mousy-looking girl. "Hey," she greets you. She peels the gum glob off the tip of her pointy nose. "How's it going?"

You check her out. Straight brown hair hangs down to her waist. A long tie-dyed skirt and tank top droop on her thin frame. You know the perfect word for this girl: "hippie"!

Your mom joins you at the door. "Are you Mary Ellen?"

"Zoe," the hippie corrects her. "From Kids-Care." She marches past you and your mom, straight into your living room. "Sorry if I'm late. Traffic was nuts. Some car went into a ditch."

"I thought our baby-sitter's name was Mary Ellen." Your mom steps toward Zoe. But then your dad honks the horn in the driveway. Your mom shrugs. "I must have heard wrong."

"No prob," Zoe says. She tucks her hair behind one ear.

Your eyes widen when you spot the tattoo of a rat on her earlobe. You've seen some strange tattoos, but a rat? Weird!

Zoe notices you looking at her ear. She quickly yanks her hair back into place. Then she smiles at your mom. "You go enjoy your weekend. Zoe will take care of everything."

For some reason, you don't like the way Zoe said that.

Turn to PAGE 3.

"Um, Mom?" you begin. Then you stop yourself. You complained all day about having a baby-sitter. You'd seem like a real baby if you confessed that Zoe makes you nervous.

"We'll be back the day after tomorrow," your mom promises. Then she gives you a hard look. "And I expect everything to go just fine here."

"Never fear, KidsCare is here," Zoe recites. She reaches into her huge shoulder bag and pulls out a bag of chips. She starts munching.

Was it your imagination, or did Zoe say "Kid-Scare"?

Zoe shuts the door behind your mom. You jump when the phone rings.

"I'll get it!" Stinko hollers. He races to the phone. "Hello!" he bleats into the receiver. "Mary Ellen? There's no Mary Ellen here. Oh, *you're* Mary Ellen. Well, that's okay. We already have a baby-sitter. Bye!" He hangs up.

"What was that about?" you ask.

"Some baby-sitter named Mary Ellen," Stinko replies. "Her car went off the road. But don't worry. I told her we already have a baby-sitter and we don't need another one."

"Mary Ellen?" you repeat.

Turn to PAGE 65.

You listen for the rats on the other side of the door. Silence. They must have gone to find a better snack!

You glance around. You're in another hallway. It's very narrow with high white walls. "That's strange," you murmur. "No roof." The walls just open to the sky.

You don't want to risk running into that pack of rats again, so you head down the hall. You hope it leads back to the main play area.

You turn left down another hall — and bang into a wall!

"Ow," you mutter, rubbing your nose. Another hall branches off to the right. You walk down that. It bends to the left.

Ten steps later you hit a dead end.

You turn and hurry back the way you came. Or the way you *think* you came. Oh, no! Another wall!

Sweat trickles down your neck.

You've lost track of where you are!

You lean against the white wall. Will you ever get out of here? How will you find Stinko and escape from the Fun Zone?

You glance up to the sky above you. Could you climb up the wall and get out the open top?

As you gaze upward, something moves into view.

Something so horrifying, you can't even scream.

Go to PAGE 36. If you dare!

A rumbling sound startles you. You spin around and see the walls of dead rats caving in on each other.

And on you.

"Help!" you scream.

At least, you *try* to scream.

But the second your mouth opens, a dead rat lands in it.

Yuck! And you thought brussels sprouts tasted bad!

Hundreds, thousands of rotting rat bodies fall, knocking you down. They pile on top of you.

You're being buried alive!

No doubt about it — you're in *grave* trouble. But don't be too discouraged. Just put this book down and try again later. And better luck next tomb!

THE END

Carefully, slowly, you ease your body out from under the rats. If they're as intelligent as your science teacher said, you figure they should be treated with respect. As you sit up, you gently remove the rats clinging to your clothing.

You shudder. You can't help it — they're creepy! But at least they're acting friendly.

You think.

A large brown rat rubs his furry head against your leg. He seems to be asking you to pet him.

"Okay, little rodent," you croon. You scratch his neck. "What do you say? Can you help me find Stinko?"

The brown rat lets out a loud squeak. The other rats swarm around you. "Hey!" you cry. "What are you rats doing?"

A few rats nudge and push you. Others pull you by your socks. They obviously want you to go forward. But why?

The rats gently herd you toward a dark hole behind the boiler in the shadows of the basement. You peek into the hole. You can't see a thing.

Should you trust these rats?

Or should you make a run for it?

If you trust them, turn to PAGE 39.
Make a run for it on PAGE 127.

"What kind of games?" you ask suspiciously.

"Games where the winner takes all," Dare drawls. "And let me warn you. I usually win."

"I want to play," Stinko pipes up. "I win a lot too."

"And what about you?" Dare turns a steely glance your way. "Do you dare to play Dare?"

"Dare, shmare," you grumble. You don't trust this guy, but you're not going to let him know he scares you.

"Sure," you declare. "I'll play. Who goes first?"

"We all go together." Dare spreads his arms wide. He swirls around and around until his tattoos blur. The colors blend into a spinning rainbow. His tattooed cape billows into the shape of a parachute.

"You know this game, I'm sure," Dare calls, still twirling. "Each of you takes hold of one side of the parachute. Then, all together, we toss it up and run under it. Only the fastest can run under and get out before the parachute comes down.

"Are you ready? On the count of three! One . . . two . . ."

To see whether or not you make it out from under the parachute, you'll need to do the puzzle on PAGE 84.

The larger of the two giant rats peers at you. "Stand back," the huge rodent commands. "We are simply correcting a terrible mistake."

You don't believe it. Not only are you being addressed by a monster-sized rat — but it actually speaks English!

"Let me explain. Once we were all ordinary lab rats," the rat continues. "Subjects in an experiment. A scientist injected us with human genes. We now have greater strength, size, and intelligence. But something went horribly wrong. Now we are trapped between being humans and being rats."

Then, right before your eyes, the other giant rat starts . . . changing.

You watch in horror as its face twists.

Bulges.

Changes color.

Collapses.

And then reshapes itself — into a new face.

A face you recognize.

Your mouth drops open.

"Zoe!" you gasp.

Shut your mouth and turn to PAGE 130.

"I don't want to play anymore," Stinko whimpers.

"Too late to change your mind now," Dare replies.

You whirl around to confront the strange baby-sitter. But you don't see him.

Where did he go?

"Looking for me?" Dare steps away from a wall. Your mouth drops open.

The tattoos on his body shift and move just like the tattoos on the wall! No wonder you didn't see him. He blends right into the walls as if he were camouflaged.

"What kind of baby-sitter are you?" you demand.

"One that likes to play by the rules," Dare answers.

"And what are the rules?" you ask.

"Simple," Dare explains. "Every game you win brings you to the next level. If you get to the highest level, you get to go home."

You stare at the tattooed man. The swirling, wriggling tattoos make you dizzy. You're almost afraid to ask your next question. "And if we don't make it that far?"

"Then I win." Dare smiles cruelly. "And you never go home. You become one of us. You join KidScare. Forever."

Turn to PAGE 49.

You stay rolled up in a ball. The thought of sinking into the plastic sea again is too scary.

You keep your chin on your chest and wrap your arms around your knees. You feel yourself bob toward the surface again.

But now something even scarier is happening. You're rising, all right — faster and faster.

Something is sucking you up to the top!

You peek out of your ball shape and see the mouth of a giant vacuum hose. One by one, scratched and dented plastic balls are being sucked up by the hose. Seconds later new balls are blown out the other end of the hose.

You try to resist.

But the force of the suction is too strong.

THWOOOOOP! You're pulled in. Warm liquid plastic sprays over you from all sides.

Now you understand. The machine recoats the balls to make them shiny and smooth again. It doesn't know you're a human being! And pretty soon, you won't know, either.

You're one of the balls now!

See you around . . . and around . . . and around!

THE END

"Gotcha!" Zoe shrieks. She springs at you and clutches you in her mutant claws.

You shrink in horror. But you don't resist. Not with all those gross rat-people lined up behind Zoe.

She shoves you and Stinko into a cage and padlocks it.

"Who are you?" you scream. "*What* are you?"

"We're the rat-people," Zoe explains. "We were created in a science experiment."

"You're ugly!" Stinko blurts.

"Stinko!" You clap your hand over his mouth.

But Zoe doesn't seem to notice. She lets out a long sigh. Her whiskers twitch. "Things used to be great. We had super strength and intelligence. And we could switch back and forth between human and giant rat. But we need to eat our special Switch Cheese formula. Otherwise, we get stuck this way. Caught between rat and human."

"Then eat the stupid formula and let us go!" you cry.

"We can't," Zoe says. "We've run out of the original batch of Switch Cheese. And we're missing one key ingredient."

Zoe presses her rat nose right up to the bars on your cage. She grins evilly. "We're missing grated kid!"

Turn to PAGE 53.

"I don't think I can make it over that wall," you confess.

"Would you rather face Zoe and the baby-sitters?" David demands.

You sigh. "You've got a point."

You grab a rope and start climbing. David climbs the rope beside you. Hand over hairy claw.

"This is like an obstacle course in the army," you huff.

"That's exactly what it is," David explains. "We all have to go through it. It's one of the tests."

Huh? What is he talking about?

But you don't have enough breath to ask.

When you reach the top, something occurs to you. "Hey," you call, jumping off the wall after David. "How did you know my baby-sitter's name is Zoe? I never told you."

"Shhhh!" David holds his claw up to his lips. He points to someone ahead of you. A figure in a military uniform.

"We're here," David announces.

The uniformed person turns around and faces you.

But it isn't a person.

It's a giant, human-sized rat!

Go to PAGE 19.

You roll an odd number on the dice. You quickly move forward that many spaces on the slate slab path. You glance down to see what this slab says.

But you're not standing on a stone slab. You're standing on a TV screen set into the sand! And instead of writing, a familiar face appears on the screen.

"It's Dare!" Stinko gasps.

Dare gazes out at you from the screen. "I always knew you were odd," he jokes. Then he winks.

The screen shakes. You and Stinko tumble off it. Into the hot white sand. "I've always found that *quick*-sand is the quickest way to end a game, haven't you?" Dare asks.

You struggle against the pull of the sand. You sink rapidly. First your ankles. Then your knees.

"No! Give us another chance!" you scream.

"Tut tut," Dare clucks. "That wouldn't be fair."

You're up to your chest . . . your chin . . . your mouth.

Just before your ears sink into the quicksand, you hear Dare's final words: "Too bad you rolled an odd number. In my games, the ODD one is always out!"

THE END

"Green," you declare, trying to sound confident. "The Beast from the East is green."

You hold your breath. Was your answer correct?

"Wrong!" the voice roars. "Everyone knows the Beast from the East is a furry blue creature. Everyone except you!"

"But . . . but . . ." you stutter.

"No buts about it!" A heavy hand slaps you hard on the shoulder.

Then the thing steps out of the shadows. At last you can see it.

It's big.

It's furry.

It's blue.

It's the Beast from the East — coming to feast on you!

THE END

The Stinko ice melts first.

"Help! Unfreeze me!" you try to say. But you can't move your lips. You're still frozen solid.

Stinko skates up to Dare. He reaches down and grabs some slush. He packs the snow and ice into a ball.

POW! Stinko wallops Dare with the snowball. "That's for scaring me!" Stinko yells.

Dare just stares icily ahead.

Then Stinko skates up to you. He has a big grin on his face. He knows you can't speak or move. "Who's the Stinko now?" he shouts right into your face. "Stinko! Stinko! Stinko!"

There's not a thing you can do about it. You're still frozen stiff.

Okay, maybe you shouldn't have called him Stinko. And maybe you teased him too much.

Your little brother is finally getting even with you. He's skating away and leaving you behind!

Just before he vanishes, he turns and sticks out his tongue.

Oh, well. Even little brothers should be able to win the game sometimes.

THE END

16

You yank open the EMPLOYEES ONLY door. A dim yellow light casts an eerie glow in the empty hallway. What's back here? you wonder. You step inside.

Better keep moving, you warn yourself. Zoe probably saw you duck in here.

You hurry along the dark corridor. No doors, no other halls to turn down, nothing. But the walls curve gently to the left. And the floor seems to slope downward.

You have the feeling you are going underground.

You come to an area with small windows along the floor. That's weird, you think. You kneel and peer down.

Your mouth drops open at the strange room below you. It looks like a scientific lab. Steel tables with sinks, Bunsen burners, test tubes — the works. And the room is full of pointy-nosed hippie girls and guys wearing white lab coats.

They all look like Zoe!

This is bizarre. How could there be so many people who look so much alike?

And just what are they studying down there underneath the Fun Zone?

Turn to PAGE 34.

"Blue!" you cry. "The Beast from the East is blue!"

"Right you are! Well done," the voice congratulates you. "Not only will I allow you to go through my cave, I will also give you a prize."

It holds something out of the shadows toward you.

You squint at it. The faint light shows you that it's an audiocassette tape.

"A tape?" You take a few steps forward. "What's on it? Music?"

"You will find out when it becomes necessary," the voice replies mysteriously. "Take it. It may help you."

You grab the tape. A shiver ripples through you.

The hand you just touched wasn't human.

It felt like a giant cat's paw!

Go to PAGE 99.

"Aaaaaaah!" you shriek. The swinging bridge hurls you headfirst over the side.

You wave your arms frantically, trying to grab hold of something — anything — to keep you from plummeting into the deep canyon.

You're in luck! Your fingers connect with the rope. You clutch it tightly.

But can you hold on? Your arm muscles burn as you reach up to the bridge with your other hand. You grab empty air. You reach again. Nothing.

Your feet dangle below you. You glance down. It's a long drop.

Whoops!

You shouldn't have looked.

Now your hand is sweating, making it hard to hold on.

You're slipping!

Hang on until PAGE 27.

You gasp in horror. But the horror mixes with anger as David salutes the giant rat!

It was a trap, you realize. David is part of this horrible nightmare.

You're too shocked even to yell at him.

"Good work, David," the rat says. "You've brought in another recruit for the rat-people's army."

Hey.

You recognize that voice.

And now that you peer closer, you recognize the face under all that rat fur.

Zoe!

Turn to PAGE 83.

You decide to quit while you're ahead.

An evil grin spreads over Dare's face. "But you aren't ahead yet," he murmurs. He winks and swirls his tattooed cape.

Your body disappears!

All that's left of you now is . . . guess what?

A HEAD!

"*Now* you can quit," Dare taunts. "While you're A HEAD!"

THE END

You wriggle your new rat body. You flick your long, thin tail.

Yup, you're a rat all right.

You just hope the rat-people know how to change you back! Maybe you should have double-checked before you agreed to switch.

"At last!" Zoe cries. "Now we'll be able to get back to being regular rats. We'll just mix their saliva into the Switch Cheese, and the formula will be complete!"

A rat-person bends down next to you and holds a cup in front of your mouth. You twitch your pointy nose and spit into the cup. You and Stinko take turns spitting until the cup is filled.

The rat leader takes the cup. He nods his giant head. "This will do. You have served your purpose." He rushes away with the cup. Dozens of rat-people scurry after him.

"Hey, wait a sec —" you call after the departing rats.

"He didn't say thank you," Stinko complains.

But you aren't thinking about the rat leader's bad manners.

Here's what you *really* want to know:

Will the rats keep their promise? Will they switch you back to your human forms?

Because you sure would like your body back now!

Turn to PAGE 112.

You decide to open the box. Dare said the only way to get home was by winning the games. Might as well get started.

"Look out!" Stinko warns. "What if something bad is in there?"

"It's just a game," you tell him.

"But what game?" Stinko asks.

You can tell he's scared. So are you.

But you're also curious.

You put your hands on the box top. Stinko leans over you, breathing down your neck. Slowly, carefully, you lift the box top off. You lean over the box to see what's inside.

You see yourself. And Stinko.

"It's a mirror!" you exclaim.

"And we're in the mirror!" Stinko adds.

"And the mirror is in the box," you hear Dare say. "And if you're in the mirror, and the mirror is in the box — well, then, I guess you're in the box too."

You and Stinko are shoved into the box. The top comes down fast! So fast, you can't fight back.

You're trapped inside. You'll never win now. Dare is finished playing THE GAME. And so are you.

THE END

You decide to stand your ground. You might as well face whatever is coming — you don't see anywhere to hide!

You step into the center of the room.

The sirens whoop louder. The lights flash faster.

And then the ground drops out from under you!

Whoa! You're sliding down a long chute. You glimpse a bright white room below you. You realize you're sliding into one of the underground labs you passed earlier.

"Man, was this ever the right decision!" you congratulate yourself. After being in that cramped, dark Rat Tomb, the white room below you looks great.

The chute levels off. You slow down, then come to a stop — inches from the mouth of the chute. You take in giant gulps of the pure, clean air.

Then, a terrifying sight freezes your breath in your lungs.

It's Stinko! Your little brother is strapped to a stainless-steel lab table. He struggles against the restraints.

But that isn't what sends chills through your body. Stinko is surrounded by hippie girls and guys.

Hippies who are half human — and half *rat*!

Slide to PAGE 109.

"What was that?" you hear Zoe demand.

"A box fell, that's all," the other girl reassures her.

You press yourself against the wall and try not to move. Which is really hard to do with dozens of gross worms inching their way up your legs. You shake your legs one at a time.

No use.

The worms cling like lint on an old sock. You want to scream, but you hold it in.

Zoe rushes over to the spilled cheese. You hold your breath and try to ignore the worms crawling across your body.

Zoe bends down and examines a hunk of worm-covered orange cheese. "Waste not, want not," she says with a grin. Then she tosses the squirming cheese into her mouth.

You gasp at the repulsive sight.

Zoe spins in your direction.

Uh-oh! You just gave yourself away!

Now what are you going to do?

Find out on PAGE 41.

There's no way you can fit through the bars.

"Stinko!" you whisper. "You've got to sneak through the bars and get those keys. It's our only chance."

"I can do it!" Stinko whispers. "I know I can!"

Your little brother slides one leg and arm between the bent bars. Then his shoulder. He turns sideways and slips the rest of the way through.

He's out!

You give him a thumbs-up. Then you point at the counter. He tiptoes over, grabs the keys, and rushes back to your cage.

"You did great!" you tell Stinko as he unlocks the cage.

You're free!

"Oh, no, you don't!" Zoe screams from the doorway.

You gulp. She is surrounded by her mutant pals. "You're not going anywhere!" she snarls.

Your eyes desperately scan the room for something, *anything* that might help you. The cages. The tables. The tape player.

You feel in your pockets. Could you have a weapon? A bribe?

Nothing. You come up empty.

Or do you?

If you have a cassette tape in your pocket, go to PAGE 116.

If your pockets are empty, go to PAGE 129.

Dare swings his cape over his ankle, on the spot where the snake tattoo had been. But before he does, you see something amazing.

Nothing.

There is absolutely nothing of Dare under the tattoo. No skin! No bones! No Dare!

Just empty space.

You're too stunned to speak.

"You may have won the game," Dare admits. "But not the match. I'll see you in your nightmares!"

With one swirl of his cape, Dare vanishes.

The ice disappears. So do the skates.

And your energy.

You and Stinko fall fast asleep.

You're snoring! Go to PAGE 47.

Just in time, a hand reaches out of the swirling orange mist. It grabs you.

"It's okay," a boy's voice reassures you. "You're safe."

Your rescuer starts to pull you back up onto the bridge. The mist is so thick that all you can see of him is a red baseball cap. And his hand clasping your wrist.

Yikes! That's no ordinary hand! A scruffy patch of fur grows across his knuckles. And his fingers aren't fingers.

They're claws.

Go to PAGE 119.

"No way!" you yell. You grab for the Instant Ice Maker. Your fingers wrap around the barrel.

"Back off!" Dare shouts.

You and Dare struggle with the spray gun. You point it at his face and squeeze the trigger.

Pssssssst! "You braaa . . . !" Dare shrieks as his mouth begins to freeze.

You spray him again. But before he freezes solid, he twists the gun around.

Psssssst! He got you! All three of you are frozen stiff.

But who's the coolest of all?

Good question. Why guess when you can find out for sure?

Take three ice cubes and three small glasses filled with hot water. Glass #1 is Stinko. Glass #2 is Dare. Glass #3 is you.

Drop a cube of ice into each glass at the same time. Which melts first?

If the Stinko ice melts first, turn to PAGE 15.

If the Dare ice melts first, turn to PAGE 108.

If your ice melts first, turn to PAGE 59.

You glance around.

No controls.

Luckily, before you panic, an engine rumbles. A vibration shakes the dome.

It must start automatically. Lucky for you!

The dome spins and twirls. You clutch your stomach. Soon it lands with a soft thump. The door slides open.

You're home!

"Well, there you are!" Your mother stands in the front door. "Did the baby-sitter leave already? Did you like her?"

Huh? What are your parents doing here?

Are they back from their trip already?

Does this mean you've been in the Fun Zone for *two days*?

Whoa . . .

"Mom," Stinko cries, "that baby-sitter was a real rat."

"Now, now," your mother scolds Stinko. "If you don't have anything nice to say . . ."

"Don't say anything at all," you finish with a wink at Stinko.

THE END

You stare around in horror. Dead rats' eyes stare back at you.

"Get me out of here!" you shriek. You leap to your feet.

The moment you stand up, lights start flashing. Alarm bells ring. The rats who led you here scatter and vanish.

"Come back!" you call after the rats. Then you realize your rat pals have betrayed you.

They led you into a trap!

The sirens blare. The lights blind you. And the awful stench is getting more intense.

You'll never be able to get out of this place before someone comes to check on the alarm. So it comes down to two choices.

Should you stand your ground in this Rat Tomb and face what is coming next?

Or should you find a place to hide?

If you stand your ground, turn to PAGE 23.
If you hide, turn to PAGE 77.

You don't have much choice, you realize. You sigh.

"Okay," you mumble. "Ask away."

"Question number one. What creature comes to life during the full moon and is part human and part animal?"

You snort. "That's easy. A werewolf!"

"Very good," the voice in the dark responds. "The next question is a little harder. High in the Himalayas lives a mysterious, furry, humanlike creature."

Ooooh! You know this one too. You saw it on *Fact or Fiction* on TV! "It's called —" you begin.

The voice cuts you off. "I want *both* names!" it warns.

You grin. "The Abominable Snowman or Yeti!" you declare. This is fun!

You hear a low rumbling sound coming from the direction of the voice. Is it a laugh? A growl?

You get nervous again.

"Now my final, and most difficult, question," the voice announces. "Although if you read GOOSE-BUMPS, it should be easy."

The voice pauses. The cave is so silent, you can almost hear your heart pounding. Finally, the voice speaks again.

"What color is the Beast from the East?"

If you think the Beast is green, turn to PAGE 14.

If you think the Beast is blue, turn to PAGE 17.

"Fun! Hooray!" Zoe cheers when your finger lands on FUN.

"Fun! Fun!" Stinko crows happily. He claps his hands.

"Whoopee," you mutter.

"Time for the fun to begin! Follow me!" Zoe orders. Adjusting her large shoulder bag, she races out the back door. Stinko grabs his red baseball cap and darts after her. You follow reluctantly.

Zoe pulls a huge silver disk out of her bag. She yanks a metal loop in the center of it. The disk opens into a dome shape. Zoe places it on the lawn. It comes up to your chest.

"Wow! Where did you get that thing?" you ask.

Zoe ignores you, touching a spot on the side of the dome. A door slides open. "Enter the DiskGo-Tech!" she commands.

"Neat!" Stinko scurries into the dome. Without giving you a chance to argue, Zoe shoves you inside. Then she crawls in after you. The door slides shut.

You have to scrunch to fit inside the cramped space. "Gee, this is too much fun for me," you grumble.

Zoe glares at you.

Then an engine rumbles. And the dome starts spinning!

"Next stop, the Fun Zone!" Zoe cries.

Turn to PAGE 71.

Oh, no! You faked it.

If you had really done the maze, you'd know that this is not an exit.

You didn't make it out!

And now you're trapped in the middle of the rat's nest!

The walls close in around you! "Aaaaahhhh!" you scream in horror. Rats squeak and scamper around you. Tiny rat claws scratch your face, your hands, through your clothes.

"Get them off!" Stinko shrieks.

Terror paralyzes you. Rats jump out of crevices and cracks in the walls. It's as if it were raining rats!

You try to cover your head. But the rats pound down on you. You and Stinko fall to the ground. You roll onto your stomach. You can't stand the idea of rats landing on your face. You struggle for breath as you feel yourself being crushed by more and more rats.

"Stinko!" you scream. "The rats are burying us alive!"

One glance tells you that Stinko knows exactly what you mean. He's under his own pile of squeaking rodents.

Oh, rats!

THE END

34

You sit back on your heels and wonder what to do next.

What's that? Your head whips around at a sound behind you.

Footsteps!

You scramble to your feet and rush down the hall. You come to a landing with several doors and a stairway. You dash down the steps two at a time.

They lead down to a storage basement. Piles of old rags, coiled ropes, and ragged nets clutter the floor. Good! Plenty of places to hide.

You hear footsteps on the floor above you. You burrow into a pile of rags. You lie very still.

Yuck! You can still feel worms wriggling around in your clothes! Eeew! They're in your hair too! You shake your head hard.

Then you freeze. From your hiding place you can hear the footsteps moving back and forth at the top of the stairs.

Will you be discovered?

Don't move! Just turn to PAGE 50.

Too bad. Your coin went over the edge of the table.

"Oh, no!" you scream. "We're going over the edge!"

The drop is sudden. You and Stinko fall faster than the speed of light.

"Whoa

aaa

aaa

aaa

aaa!" you both cry as you drop down,

down,

down.

"Where are we going?" Stinko cries.

"Nowhere!" Dare's voice booms all around you. "You're going Nowhere — fast!"

THE END

Your mouth drops wide open. But no sound comes out.

You blink over and over. Your brain tries to make sense of what you are seeing. It is impossible — but very real.

A giant rat peers down at you.

Holding a clipboard.

And wearing a white lab coat.

"No!" you whisper. You stumble backwards down the hallway.

The rat follows you along the top of the wall.

You come to another dead end. "No! No!" you scream. You pound your fists on the wall.

Then you glance up again.

The rat is taking notes!

You race through the twisting corridors. First this way, then that. No escape! Just hallways leading to more hallways.

With growing horror you realize: You're in a giant maze.

This time, *you're* the experiment!

You sink to the ground. Will you ever find the way out of this crazy maze?

Sorry. Not in this lifetime. Everywhere you turn only brings you to a

DEAD END.

"Now's our chance, Stinko!" You grab Stinko and dash through the door in the castle wall. You glance back to see if Dare is following you.

WHAM! You smash right into a marble column. Your head spins from the impact.

A door in the long, narrow column opens up. You and Stinko tumble into a Plexiglas tube.

The tube snaps shut. The column door slides closed. You and Stinko are sealed in the tube!

"It's like the money tube at the drive-in bank!" Stinko exclaims.

Exactly.

WHOOSH!

The tube — with you and Stinko in it — is swiftly sucked up by a strong force. A whirring sound surrounds you. You're speeding through a dark tunnel.

All this has happened so fast, you haven't had time to think about what's waiting at the end of this tube trip.

If there is an end . . .

Go to PAGE 70.

"Stinko!" you call after the kid heading for the cave. But he disappears through the opening. You dart after him.

"Hey, you brat!" an angry voice behind you shouts. "Where do you think you're going?"

Oops. Maybe you were supposed to pay an admission fee. Unfortunately, you don't have any money. "I need a bigger allowance," you mutter. You speed up.

You reach the cave. A sign over the entrance reads: TO WEIRD WOODS. You dash in and then out the other side.

"Whoa, cool!" you exclaim. You gaze around.

The huge area looks exactly like a jungle. It is so realistic, you wonder if you're still indoors! Jungle sounds and smells surround you. Thick orange mist rises from a deep canyon. You spot a narrow rope bridge disappearing into the mist.

You don't see Stinko, though.

But, wait — is that a red baseball cap bobbing across the rope bridge?

You dash onto the bridge. A little too quickly. The wobbly rope bridge sways and swings. Faster. And faster.

You struggle desperately to keep your balance. No use! You're going to fall!

Go to PAGE 18.

You decide to trust the rats. They're not hurting you. In fact, they're very friendly. Maybe they're going to show you the way out.

Squeaking softly, the rats head into the dark hole. You follow them down a chilly, spooky tunnel. A strong, bad odor fills your nostrils. The smell of something rotting hangs thick in the air.

As your eyes adjust to the darkness, you get a better look at your surroundings. You realize this isn't just an empty tunnel. Narrow shafts of light shine in through cracks in the walls. But the walls aren't ordinary walls.

They're walls of mummified rats!

A dim light shines on an engraved plaque. You kneel down beside it. Your heart pounds as you read the words out loud.

"'TOMB OF THE UNKNOWN RATS — Here lie the innocent Rats of Lab. Their deaths shall be remembered . . .'"

The next words catch in your throat. "'And *revenged*!'" you gasp.

Get a grip on yourself and turn to PAGE 30.

You gasp! You can't believe Dare's palm just disappeared like that!

You lean forward to get a closer look at his invisible palm. Dare doesn't try to hide it from you. In fact, he holds it out for you to see.

"Here," he says. "Have a good look. It won't bite you." He shoves his hand inches from your face.

Yikes! A vampire bat pokes its head through the hole left by the disappearing rat.

Before you can pull back, the bat's fangs dig into your neck. A warm, woozy feeling rushes through you.

Uh-oh. You've been bitten by a vampire.

You know what that means.

You're a vampire too!

Go to PAGE 82.

Zoe peeks around the cheese boxes. Her eyes narrow when she sees you.

"You little brat!" she growls. She reaches for you.

You shove the stack of wormy cheese boxes onto her. Cheese flies everywhere. She's covered with cheese crumbs and zillions of worms.

You don't waste a minute. You race toward an EXIT sign in the distance.

"Get that kid!" Zoe screams through her mask of worms. The other hippie girl trips over the cheese boxes. You've got a good head start, you tell yourself.

But when you reach the EXIT sign, you discover it's not really an exit. It actually says: *NO* EXIT. EMPLOYEES ONLY.

Next to the door is one of the dark cave entrances. Over it a sign announces: THIS WAY TO WEIRD WOODS.

You glance behind you. Zoe is catching up. And she's not alone! Choose!

If you go through the EMPLOYEES ONLY door, turn to *PAGE 16*.

If you dash into the cave toward *Weird Woods*, turn to *PAGE 80*.

"Ready or not," you shout, "here I come!"

You jump into the pit. Immediately you start sinking. Hard plastic balls bounce off your face, neck, and arms. The air between the balls is full of static electricity. It smells like old Barbie dolls.

"Help!" you scream. Layers and layers of colored balls close in around your face. You can't breathe. You're drowning in a sea of colored balls. You don't know how to swim in plastic!

But maybe you can float in it!

You tuck your chin to your chest. You bring in your arms and legs and scrunch up into a ball.

It's working! You're not sinking anymore!

You start to rise to the surface. You peek out from your ball shape and spot Stinko a few feet ahead of you.

But as soon as you uncurl, you immediately begin to sink again.

Now what should you do? Stinko's getting away from you!

If you stay rolled up in a ball, roll to PAGE 10.
If you uncurl and go after your brother, swim to PAGE 113.

"Down!" you cry.

The LOBBY button lights up. The elevator motor whirs.

You hear rats scratching at the elevator door. Relief floods over you as the elevator starts moving down.

You watch the numbers above the door: 16. 15. 14.

"Whew! I didn't think we'd make it," you admit. "That was really close!"

"How close was it?"

Uh-oh. That wasn't Stinko's voice.

You feel hot breath on the back of your neck. The voice speaks again. "Was it this close?"

You whirl around and come face-to-face with Dare.

What's left of Dare, that is.

Go to PAGE 52.

PUHHHH!

You and Stinko pop out of the Plexiglas drainpipe and land with a thud. A few more kids drop out of the pipe after you.

You glance around. You're in a big, windowless, white room. Loud rock music blasts from a black boom box sitting on a stainless-steel counter.

But over the music you hear cries and moans. Where are those terrible wails coming from? you wonder.

Your eyes land on rows of cages lining one wall.

A scream stops in your throat.

The cages are full of kids!

Then a figure steps out from behind a white screen. A sight more terrifying than the caged humans.

A giant rat!

Go to PAGE 131.

Congratulations! You and Stinko easily dash under and out of the giant parachute before it lands on you.

"Excellent." Dare nods his tattooed head. "I'm looking forward to beating you at my games."

You glance around. Nothing looks familiar. In fact, everything looks very, very strange! The trees are orange! The grass is purple!

You're not in your house anymore, that's for sure!

"Wh-wh-where are we?" you stammer.

"Right where I want you to be." Dare hurls his tattooed cape at you. It drops onto you and Stinko.

You and Stinko back up quickly. But the cape is quicker. It closes down around you. You try to lift one edge.

It won't budge.

When you look around for Dare, you don't spot him anywhere. All you see are tattoos of snakes, spiders, dragons, and rats — wriggling and writhing on the walls around you.

"Look out!" Stinko cries. "The tattoos are alive!"

Stinko is right. This is a tattooed tent of terror.

And you and Stinko are trapped inside!

Go to PAGE 9.

46

Two giant rats stand in the center of the Tomb. Rats the size of humans!

They're wearing lab coats.

And standing on their hind legs.

You burrow deeper into the rat wall. These rats may be dead and disgusting, but at least they're not enormous mutants!

The two hideous rats sniff around the Tomb. They gaze at each other and shrug.

Then they turn and leave the Tomb.

You slide out of the wall of dead rats. "How can it be?" you moan. "What kind of crazy place is this?"

You have to escape. You and Stinko are in terrible danger. Rats that trick you, walls of dead rats, and now *giant* rats!

And it all began with Zoe. The baby-sitter with the rat tattoo on her ear.

Figure it out later! you scold yourself. Move it — *now!*

You peer down the Tomb's long corridor. A steel gate is sliding down at the opening at the end of the hall! *Oh, no!*

The rats are sealing the Tomb!

Turn to PAGE 5.

As soon as you fall asleep, you dream.

In your dream, you and Stinko are neck deep in swirling water. On one side of the water, the dragon tattoo from Dare's cape stands ready to blast you with its flaming breath.

On the other side of the water, a stone castle casts a shadow over you.

You're in a moat encircling the castle. You look up and see Dare gazing down from a turret. The dragon's breath sends you and Stinko swimming as fast and hard as you can.

Dare laughs.

Guess what?

This isn't a dream.

This is the nightmare Dare said he would see you in!

Go to PAGE 51.

You stare, horrified, at the claw in the ceiling. It scrapes at the hole. The claw is almost all the way through.

"Is this an emergency?" Stinko cries.

"Of course it is, dumbo!" you snap. Your mind races, trying to think of a way out of this mess.

Stinko jumps up and slaps his hand against the elevator's control panel. The elevator comes to a screeching halt.

"Aaaaaaiiiieeee!" A bloodcurdling squeal rises and then falls away. Whatever was breaking through the ceiling is gone now. The sudden stop must have thrown it off the top of the elevator!

"What did you do?" you shout at Stinko.

"You said it was an emergency," he replies, looking offended. "So I pushed the emergency button."

Laughing, you give Stinko a grateful hug.

Whoa. Get a grip!

You let go immediately.

"Come on, Stinko," you say, pushing another button. "We've got to get out of here!"

If you pushed the FUN AND GAMES KIDSCARE OFFICES button, go to PAGE 73.

If you pushed the LOBBY button, go to PAGE 43.

"That's not fair!" you yell. "You never told us that!"

"You never asked." Dare shrugs. Which makes the pictures swirling around on his body look even weirder.

Stinko stomps his foot. "Take me home right now!" he demands.

"The only way home is through the games," Dare says.

He steps back — and disappears into the tattooed walls.

A large flat box appears in the spot where he was standing. On the box top are the words THE GAME BOX.

As you gaze at it, you shiver. A cold wind blows through the tent. It lifts one tattooed edge slightly.

If you grab Stinko and run to the open edge of the tent, turn to PAGE 96.

If you open the box, go to PAGE 22.

You force yourself to stay still. You wait.

And wait.

And wait.

Soon, your eyes close.

"Ouch!" Your own cry wakes you from a deep sleep. Something is pinching you all over. No. Something is *biting* you!

The dim light reveals a horrifying sight. You're covered in a living blanket of . . .

Rats!

Hundreds of huge, scaly-tailed, sharp-toothed, pointy-nosed rats!

Uh-oh. Better turn to PAGE 132. Fast!

"Swim, Stinko!" you yell.

But Stinko's too scared to move. He holds on to your leg. He's dragging you down into the freezing water. If you don't start swimming, you'll go under!

You stretch both arms forward in your best butterfly stroke to escape the fiery breath of the dragon. You're in luck! A low drawbridge spans the moat in front of you.

You reach for the side of it. The bridge rises slowly, carrying you and Stinko with it.

Then the drawbridge stops midway. The dragon shoots fire, just missing Stinko's feet.

"Aahhhhh!" Stinko screams as he dangles from your ankles.

Your arm muscles are stretched to the limit. You don't think you can hold on much longer.

"I'm waiting for you!" Dare calls down.

The dragon breathes fire again. The flames lick at your legs. Yeoww! That's hot!

You could try to pull yourself up and out of its way. Or you could drop to cool the fire in the moat below.

If you try to pull yourself and Stinko onto the bridge, go to PAGE 126.

If you drop back into the moat, go to PAGE 89.

You gasp in horror. Stinko cowers in the corner.

A grotesque figure stands inches from you in the elevator. It's Dare.

But a very different Dare!

Whole pieces of his body are missing. A knee. An arm. One ear. Half his face. Part of a shoulder.

Where tattoos once were, there is nothing now. Just air.

The tattoos hid the fact that Dare is nothing without them. Every time you won a game, Dare lost a tattoo. And he also used some up trying to defeat you.

The tattoos that are left are in trouble too. Tattered creatures gasp for breath. They struggle to hang on to each other. To keep a shape, a form. To stick together. To keep Dare alive.

"The game is almost over," Dare growls. "I'm losing the games. I'm losing everything. I'm supposed to be the winner. These are my games. And I want to win my games!"

Go to PAGE 95.

You leap back from the bars.

"Grated kid?" you gasp. "What's that?"

"Exactly what it sounds like, genius," Zoe answers.

Stunned, you sink to your knees. Stinko covers his head with his arms and whimpers. The kids in the other cages moan.

"We'll make the necessary preparations." Zoe sets a ring of keys down on the counter and leads the way out the door. The other mutants follow her. You stare after them.

That's when you notice one of the bars in the cage is bent.

Could you — or Stinko — possibly slip through?

If you could get those keys, you could open all the cages. It's probably your only chance to save your life.

But you don't have much time.

You study the bars.

Don't think about it too long! Get moving! They'll be back any minute!

If you try to slip through the bars yourself, turn to PAGE 114.

If you send Stinko instead, turn to PAGE 25.

"I choose ALL!" you declare. "I want ALL."

You keep your eyes on Dare's shriveling, tattooed face. You wait to see his reaction.

You don't have to wait long. A smile spreads across his hideous, crumbling mouth.

"Did you say ALL?" he asks.

You nod fearfully.

"Then ALL it is!"

With the wink of his green eye and a blink of his blue eye, ALL Dare's tattoos are back on his body.

ALL your winning games are lost.

ALL your memories of the last hours are gone.

You lose the most dangerous game.

But ALL is not lost! Turn to PAGE 100 and start the games

ALL

OVER

AGAIN!

Maybe David is just a nice kid with a claw. Who knows? But you're not taking any chances. You decide to go your own way.

"Sorry, David," you say, "I'd rather take my chances on my own."

You take a few steps backwards. Then you add, "Uh, thanks for saving me. And good luck!"

Just because the kid is creepy doesn't mean you can't be polite.

You turn around, facing the rope bridge again. Zoe and the other baby-sitters are hidden in the mist somewhere near the middle of the bridge.

Maybe you could sneak by them. The orange mist is so thick, they might not see you.

You step onto the bridge. Immediately it sinks a little lower and starts to swing.

Can you make it past the baby-sitters and across the swinging bridge? Or should you try to find another way back to Stinko?

If you take the bridge route, turn to PAGE 123.
If you look for another way back to Stinko, turn to PAGE 107.

For once Stinko listens. He follows you willingly.

You have no idea where you're going. You just run as fast as you can, gripping Stinko's wrist tightly. Your eyes dart all around, desperately searching for a way out.

Zoe the rat-girl chases you. "What are you doing here?" she screams. "This is Fun! You're supposed to be in Games!"

You glance back at her. Yikes! An army of giant rats surrounds Zoe.

"After them!" Zoe cries. "Don't let them get away!"

You and Stinko run as fast as you can. You can tell he's getting tired. He's panting hard.

But you have to keep going. Zoe and the rat pack are gaining on you.

"Run!" you beg Stinko. "Run for your life!"

With the rats close behind, you come to a wall. Two elevator doors open at the same time. One is going up. One is going down.

"Which one should we get on?" Stinko cries.

You have no idea. But your life depends on it. Hurry!

Flip a coin. If the coin lands heads up, go up to PAGE 118.

If the coin lands heads down, go down to PAGE 43.

Knowing Stinko, he's definitely headed for the Bottomless Ball Pit. You follow the kid in the red cap who's running in that direction.

Good choice. It's Stinko, all right.

Before you can catch up to him, he reaches the edge of the ball pit. "Stinko!" you holler at him. "Get back here, you dumbo!"

Stinko glances over at you and sticks out his tongue. "I don't have to," he taunts. "You're not my boss!"

Typical Stinko.

You open your mouth to scream again. Too late. He dives. He lands in the middle of the colored plastic balls.

And vanishes!

Get over the urge to leave your little brother behind. Then go to PAGE 128.

You choose red.

Of course you would choose red. Red is always a vampire's favorite color. And now that you're a vampire, red is your favorite color too.

The bite of the vampire is working. Your human shape changes to the shape of a vampire bat. Your perfect teeth change into fangs. And your bedtime changes from night to day.

What can you say at a time like this?

Just one thing.

"Fangs, Dare. Fangs a lot."

THE END

Your ice melted first. You're free!

You stare at the Dare ice statue. His mouth is frozen open in a snarl. His tattooed arms are raised. His hands are balled into tattooed fists. Even frozen in ice, Dare looks scary.

"Boy, oh boy," you mutter. "We are going to be in big trouble when Dare thaws." You have to get Stinko and escape before Dare's ice coat melts.

Stinko is still a frozen kidsicle. You take off one of your ice skates. Using the blade of the skate, you chip away at the ice on Stinko's face.

"Get me out of this icebox!" Stinko shouts as soon as his mouth is free.

For a second you wish you'd left his mouth frozen shut. "All right, all right," you snap. "I'm going as fast as I can. Just a few more chips and you'll be free."

"No!" Stinko gasps.

"Yes!" you argue. "Quit moving, or the blade will —"

You can't finish your sentence. An icy tattooed hand reaches around and clamps over your mouth.

"That's what I was trying to tell you," Stinko cries. "Dare broke out of the ice!"

Turn to PAGE 64.

60

You swallow hard. "Okay, we'll do it," you announce.

You can't help feeling sorry for the rat-people. After all, you think, humans got them into this mess. You feel as if it's your duty as a human to get them out of it.

If you can . . .

"Come on, Stinko," you say, undoing the straps that hold your little brother down on the table. "We're going to help them get back to their normal forms."

"You mean we have to eat that cheese?" Stinko whines. "But it stinks!"

"Think of it as medicine," Zoe suggests. She holds out the cheese. "One little bite each. That's all it takes."

"Well, here goes," you say. You hope you sound braver than you feel. You close your eyes, hold your nose, and take a bite.

Stinko follows your lead.

Instantly the two of you start changing. Fur covers your bodies. Claws replace your hands and feet. Whiskers sprout around your newly pointy noses. You and Stinko flop down to all fours.

You don't believe it, but it's true.

You and Stinko are rats!

Go to PAGE 21.

You figure Stinko will be fine playing in the Fun Zone. In fact, he'll probably be furious when you try to get him to leave. It's more important to find out what Zoe has to say.

You spot a stack of boxes. Quickly, you duck behind them. As you crouch down, you notice they are marked SWITCH CHEESE.

Hmm. You frown. Must mean Swiss cheese.

Oops! Your shoulder knocks against a box. You try to grab it, but it crashes to the floor. It breaks open.

Yecch! A horrible stench fills the air. Rotting rounds of orange cheese roll from the boxes.

Thousands of fat, slimy white worms wriggle out of the cheese and squirm at your feet.

Oh — gross!

Turn to PAGE 24.

"A sand monster!" Stinko cries.

So Stinko sees it too. It's real.

A monstrous blob is rising out of the sand. It rolls toward you like a sandstorm.

As the creature comes nearer, you notice a black hole in its shapeless center. Sand is sucked into the hole with the force of a cyclone wind. Anything in the Sand Blob's path is sure to be drawn into that giant black hole.

"We've got to get out of here!" you shout.

But Stinko is too terrified. He throws himself down on the slate slab and covers his head with his arms.

You yank at his shirt. "Come on!" you insist. "Get up!"

Stinko suddenly sits up, feeling the slab with his fingers. "There's writing on this," he exclaims. "Look!"

Stinko's right! There are letters carved into it! "Roll the dice to make your next move," you read aloud.

A pair of dice appear at your feet.

"It's another game," you whisper. "A game of chance!"

Feeling lucky? Roll a pair of dice to find your next move.

If you roll an even number, go to PAGE 86.

If you roll an odd number, go to PAGE 13.

KERPLOP!

You land in the gloppy yellow gunk. Yuck! It goes up your nose. It glues your eyes shut. And the goo is almost impossible to move through.

You kick hard. Your pants hook on something at the bottom of the cheese pool. It whips you back and forth like a blade in a blender — and you've been set on puree!

The blender blade swirls faster and faster. You feel sick as you realize what's happening. What you're being made into.

You have enough air to shout your very last words.

"Gee whiz!"

No, not *gee whiz*.

CHEESE WHIZ!

THE END

64

You wrestle free of Dare's hand and turn to face him. You gape at the hideous sight.

One by one the tattoos on his body are thawing out. The cyclone spins again. The shrunken Cyclops head swings back and forth. Poisonous spiders, vampire bats, venomous snakes, and rabid rats come to life.

"My tattooed friends don't enjoy the cold," Dare declares.

From the way the tattoos are staring at you, you believe him.

"And I don't like the way you played that last game," Dare snarls. "We'll have to do something about that!"

Go to PAGE 98.

That's strange, you think. You turn to face Zoe. "Mary Ellen was the name Mom —"

"Forget it," Zoe cuts you off. "We've got better things to do than worry about some bad driver named Mary Ellen."

"Like what?" you grumble. You're already sure you're going to be bored this whole weekend.

"Like this!" Zoe reaches into her huge bag and pulls out a giant game spinner.

"Whoah!" Stinko exclaims. "What's that?"

You don't want to seem too interested, but you can't help peeking at it out of the corner of your eye.

The first thing you notice is a silhouette of a rat in the center. Just like the tattoo on Zoe's ear!

This girl has rats on the brain, you think.

You move forward to get a closer look. The spinner is divided into two sections. One section says FUN. The other section says GAMES.

"It's up to you now." Zoe holds the spinner in front of you. "What happens next is your choice. What's it going to be? Fun or games?"

Turn to the Spinner on PAGE 136.

If your finger stops on FUN, turn to PAGE 32.

If your finger stops on GAMES, turn to PAGE 100.

66

"Fine," you mutter. "We'll find our own way out." You glance around the stone castle.

Okay, you think, we can't go out the door. It's bolted tight.

Your eyes land on stone steps leading down into the cellar.

"This way, Stinko," you whisper. You dart down the stairs.

They bring you to a dark tunnel. Maybe it's a passageway under the moat! You begin to run. . . .

And then . . . you stop.

Hundreds of glittering eyes stare at you from the darkness.

"Yikes!" you shriek. "Rats!"

"Nooooo!" Stinko screams. "Get me out of here!"

"I'm trying! I'm trying!" You grab him by his sleeve and drag him behind you. Rats scurry from under your feet. They nip at your ankles as you dash through the dark tunnel.

You turn left — and come to a solid wall. You go back, turn right — and come to another solid wall.

"Stinko," you gasp. "I think we're trapped in a maze!"

Look over at PAGE 67.

Yup. It *is* a maze!

Use a pencil to find your way through it. Put your pencil point at START. Do not lift your pencil up until you are out of the maze. Then follow the directions at the end.

Start

Go to page 33

Run to page 103

You grab one of the ropes and swing across the pit. But you use too much force. You swing out beyond the sea of colored balls below you.

Uh-oh. You forgot the old saying, "Look before you leap." On the other side of the pit is a huge vat of swirling orange-yellow goop. A sign on the vat says SWITCH CHEESE.

You swing back to the side you started from. Then you swing over the cheese vat again. And then back.

As you swing back and forth, you gaze down, trying to spot Stinko in the ball pit.

Whoa. You're over the vat again. And your grip is slipping.

Make that slipped!

Plunge to PAGE 63.

"What a pain!" you mutter. You push through the turnstile to tell Zoe what happened. After all, she's the baby-sitter. Let *her* deal with Stinko.

Zoe is talking to another girl — another girl in hippie clothes. The baby-sitter is so deep in conversation that she didn't even notice Stinko's mad dash into the Fun Zone.

The two hippie girls are laughing about something. As you get closer, you hear what they're saying.

"Getting rid of Mary Ellen was easy," Zoe boasts. "The old giant-rat-in-the-road trick. Made her swerve into a ditch. Works every time. Now the two brats are ours!"

A shudder runs through you. What could Zoe be talking about? She sounds crazy. And dangerous!

Don't panic, you tell yourself. There must be an explanation for what Zoe just said.

Should you listen to find out what else this weird baby-sitter will say? Or do you go after Stinko yourself and get out of here?

If you stay to hear more, turn to PAGE 61.
If you go after Stinko, turn to PAGE 79.

70

THUD! The speeding tube stops. Your stomach got lost somewhere back in the tunnel, but now it catches up to you again.

The door on the tube flies open.

Stinko rushes out first. "Wow!" he exclaims. He points to a neon sign hanging over an entrance gate to an indoor playground. The sign says KIDSCARE FUN ZONE.

"There's Zoe! Our real baby-sitter!" Stinko yells, pointing at a thin girl in a droopy tank top. "Hey, Zoe! We're over here!"

Zoe turns to see who's calling her name.

But when she turns around, your eyes widen at the horrifying sight.

From the back, she looks like Zoe.

From the front, she looks like a giant rat!

"Come on, Stinko," you gasp, grabbing your brother by the neck of his shirt. "She's not a real baby-sitter. And something tells me the Fun Zone isn't really fun!"

Run to PAGE 56.

This isn't fun at all! You feel dizzy and nauseous. Luckily, the spinning stops before you toss your cookies.

The door slides open. You hear organ music and kids screaming. The smell of Nachos fills the air.

"Awesome! Thanks, Zoe!" Stinko runs out of the dome.

You exit slowly, trying to regain your balance — and your lunch! "Where are we?" you ask.

Zoe points to a yellow neon sign.

"'KidScare Fun Zone,'" you read aloud.

KidScare?

Hmmm . . .

You gaze at the huge indoor playground in front of you. Just beyond the turnstiles, kids jump into an Olympic pool-sized pit, filled with colorful plastic balls.

Baby stuff, you think. But the slides aimed down tubes that look like tornado funnels seem kind of fun. And the pitch-dark cave entrances dotting the far walls look cool.

"Wait here," Zoe orders. "I have to check in."

Zoe strolls through a turnstile. A second later, Stinko dashes behind Zoe into the play area.

"Stinko!" you shout. "Get back here, you dumbo!"

Go to PAGE 69.

Good! You choose yellow. The color of the sun. Vampires hate the sun.

You open up the sunny-colored ball. A beam of sunshine darts out.

That's all it takes to destroy the vampire in you. One look at the ray of sunshine and you're cured! Saved!

The sunbeam zooms across the room — and lights up a secret door hidden in the castle wall.

"Look, Stinko!" you cry. "That might be the way out!"

Before you can move toward the door, Dare speaks. "You win this round," he tells you.

"I do?" you sputter with surprise. "But I expected —"

"Expect the unexpected in all my games," Dare interrupts you. "You're doing very well, for a beginner."

You peer at Dare suspiciously. Is he actually being nice?

"In fact, you're so good, I'm going to give you a choice," Dare continues.

Here it is:

To quit while you're ahead, turn to PAGE 20.
To go through the secret door, turn to PAGE 37.

You pushed the Fun and Games KidScare Offices button. The elevator starts moving up again. Air whistles through the hole in the ceiling where the claw broke through.

In a few seconds the elevator stops. The door slides open. You poke out your head. "All clear," you tell Stinko. You and Stinko step out into a large open area. The elevator door closes behind you and disappears.

"That's weird," you murmur, glancing around. There are no windows here. No doors.

No way out.

The only furniture is a desk sitting in the middle of the huge empty space. You step cautiously over to it.

On the desk is an answering machine. The red light on the machine is flashing. There's a message.

You can't help it. You push PLAY.

Get the message on PAGE 135.

Zoe's face writhes and contorts. Then she's a rat again.

"You see the problem?" she cries. "We can't stop switching. We need help. We developed Switch Cheese as a cure. But it doesn't work right."

"I don't know anything about making cheese," you protest. "And Stinko doesn't know anything about anything!"

"I heard that!" Stinko complains from the table.

"It's your makeup," Zoe explains.

"Makeup! I don't wear makeup!" you scoff. "And if Stinko wears makeup, it's news to me!"

"Your *genetic* makeup," Zoe corrects you. "You two have the right genes to become rats. With a little scrambling."

You shake your head. "I'd believe that about Stinko, but in my case you've got the wrong kid."

"I heard that too!" Stinko whines.

"You're the right kids. We're sure." Zoe approaches you. "All you and Stinko have to do is eat a little Switch Cheese. A few nibbles — and we'll have the results we need."

You're almost afraid to ask. But you have to. "And what might those results be?"

Zoe smiles. "You and Stinko will become rats."

Go to PAGE 88.

Dare stands in front of you. The spotlights shine right through his invisible spots. The hot lights make the remaining tattoo creatures squirm. The only sounds are the sounds of the creatures hissing, gasping, dying slowly.

Dare takes off his T-shirt. A hulking, horned beast tattoo rears its head on his chest.

The beast roars, baring a mouthful of flesh-ripping teeth!

Stinko screams in terror. You throw your arms up to protect your face.

When Dare laughs, you can see right through the back of his head!

"The last game is deadly simple," he explains. "Only one of us can win. Only one of us can survive. It is the most dangerous game of all."

Your throat is so dry with fear, you can't speak. "But what do I do?" you whisper.

"You simply make a choice," Dare tells you. "You look at me and make a choice. All or Nothing. It's that simple."

Go to PAGE 105.

You'll take the path. Forget the cave. Who knows what trouble you might find in there? It's better to just keep going. That Bottomless Ball Pit must be right up ahead somewhere.

As you round a big rock, you hear the screams and squeals of kids. You run toward the sounds.

There it is! The Bottomless Ball Pit!

Then you spot a kid in a red baseball cap standing on the edge of the pit. About to jump in.

It's Stinko!

"Stinko!" you scream to him.

He turns, looks at you, and waves. Then he jumps into the pit.

And sinks like a stone!

Go to PAGE 128.

Hide! You may be brave, but you're not *stupid*!

You glance around the rat-lined Tomb. Yikes! There's only one place to hide.

In the wall.

The wall of rats.

You touch the lifeless, furry rat bodies. "Ugh!" you moan in disgust. You try not to breathe the dead-rat air as you push open a space between the piled-up bodies.

You slide into the space. The little bodies fold back over you. You are completely hidden except for your eyes and nose.

Two figures wearing white coats enter the Tomb. You can't quite see them from your hiding place. Their backs are to you.

One turns off the flashing lights.

The other shuts down the siren.

Then they turn around.

You have to bite the inside of your cheek to keep from screaming.

Ouch! Head to PAGE 46.

Whew! You win. Your coin stopped just short of the edge.

You breathe a sigh of relief. You yank Stinko away from the edge. The tent reappears.

Huh? How?

You don't care how it happened. You crawl inside, dragging Stinko in with you. Anywhere is better than Nowhere!

You stand up. The tent's walls and ceiling vanish!

"Where are we now?" Stinko asks.

"I don't know," you murmur, gazing around.

You're standing on a slab of slate. It's one of many slabs forming a path through endless white sand. The pure white sand blankets the ground as far as your eye can see.

A burning ball of fire shines brightly overhead. Stinko wipes sweat from his forehead. "Are we at the beach?" he asks.

It's more like a desert! A broiling wave of heat hits your face. You gaze out toward distant dunes and squint your eyes.

You struggle to focus on something too strange to be real.

In the middle of the heat, you feel a chill.

Am I really seeing that? you wonder.

Or are my eyes playing tricks on me?

Go to PAGE 62.

You decide to go after Stinko yourself. Zoe gives you the creeps. You just want to get out of here. But before you can get *out*, you've got to get *in* and fetch your little brother!

While Zoe's back is turned, you crawl under the turnstile. Standing up, you glance around. You don't see Stinko anywhere. Where did that little brat go? you wonder.

"Stinko!" you yell. But there's no way he can hear you over the music and screaming kids.

Then you spot a familiar red baseball cap in the distance. Stinko! All you can see is the hat — in a crowd of kids standing at the edge of a swimming pool. A swimming pool filled with colored plastic balls. A big sign overhead reads: BOTTOMLESS BALL PIT.

You would recognize that hat anywhere.

Or would you?

You glimpse another red baseball cap. On the head of another kid.

And this kid is heading toward one of the caves! Which kid is Stinko?

If you follow the kid heading for the cave, go to PAGE 38.

If you think the kid at the ball pit is Stinko, turn to PAGE 57.

You dash through the cave and step out into an enormous jungle setting. Plastic rocks jut out like cliffs. Fake plants tower overhead. Exotic smells and sounds fill the air.

Awesome! you think. This Fun Zone building must be huge!

Right in front of you, a bridge stretches across a deep, dark canyon. A thick mist makes it impossible for you to see where the bridge leads. Or what might be on the other side.

But Zoe is definitely on *this* side. Glancing back, you see her racing toward you. "Not that way!" she cries.

So she doesn't want you going over the bridge. Then that's just what you'll do! You step onto the wobbly rope floor. It shakes so badly, you almost fall over the side!

Hmmmm. Maybe this was a bad idea.

"Get back here, you brat!" Zoe yells at you.

No way, you think. She is one rotten baby-sitter!

You dart along the shaky rope bridge. After you've gone about halfway, it begins to sway back and forth.

You clutch the rope railings. You feel as if you're riding a wild ride at an amusement park.

Only, you're not amused!

You're losing your footing. You're losing your grip!

Oh, no! You're going to fall!

Turn to PAGE 18.

All that is left of Dare is air. The tattoos are all gone. The beastly baby-sitter is a horrible thing of the past.

And Stinko is the only tattoo that survived.

It's all over.

Finally!

"Ready to go home now, Stinko?" you ask, ruffling your brother's hair.

"I'm not a Stinko!" your brother argues.

"Are too."

"Am not!"

"Are too."

"Am not!"

"Are too!"

Oh, well.

Some things never

END.

"Are you okay?" Stinko asks.

"I-I think so . . ." you reply. So far, you don't feel any different.

"I lied. It did bite after all." Dare laughs. "But you don't have to turn into a vampire if you play the game right."

"This is no time for games!" you cry.

"It's always time for games," Dare scolds.

He tosses three balls into the air and starts juggling. "Inside one of these balls you'll find a cure," he explains. "All you have to do is guess which ball. Is it the red ball? Is it the yellow ball? Or is it the green ball?"

Dare keeps juggling while you try to decide which ball will save you.

Turn to the Spinner on PAGE 136. Follow the directions at the top of the page.

If your finger lands on green, turn to PAGE 121.

If your finger lands on red, turn to PAGE 58.

If your finger lands on yellow, turn to PAGE 72.

"You deserve a reward," Zoe the rat continues. "Come forward for your Switch Cheese."

David steps forward and takes the cheese from Zoe's outstretched claw. He pops it into his mouth. Your eyes widen as you watch the incredible changes taking place.

More fur grows on David's clawed hand. His face narrows and becomes pointy. Whiskers sprout under his new nose. His eyes turn beady and black.

Now David is more rat than kid!

"Your turn." Zoe holds a piece of Switch Cheese toward you. "This cheese will turn you into one of us. Then you can join our army."

You stare at her.

"It will be easier on you if you do as I say," Zoe warns. "We're taking over."

If you decide to join the rat-people's army, turn to PAGE 104.

If you refuse to eat the cheese, turn to PAGE 115.

Pick a string, any string. Follow it to an end. What you do *next* will depend on what you do *now*.

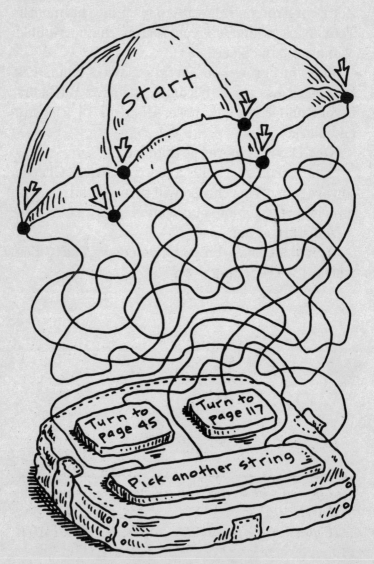

"Why don't we go back the same way we got here?" Stinko suggests. He reaches under a lab table, then holds up Zoe's large shoulder bag.

"Hey, Stinko," you say. "You're not as dumb as you look." You grab the bag and open it.

There it is. The DiskGo-Tech.

You yank up the loop in the center of the disk. It pops up to a dome. You press on all the edges. A door slides open.

"Wow!" Stinko shouts. "You did it!"

"Don't I keep telling you I'm a genius?" you joke. "Now hurry. Get inside." You have a creepy feeling that if you don't leave right away, some other mutants may show up and try to use you for some other weird experiments.

You crawl after Stinko into the DiskGo-Tech dome.

"Make it go!" Stinko urges.

"I will, I will!"

But how?

Can you make it work? Turn to PAGE 29 to see.

You roll an even number on the dice.

Before you can even ask what comes next, a deafening roar fills your ears. Hot wind whips around you. A cyclone funnel like the tattoo on Dare's shoulder sucks you forward. You and Stinko bounce onto the next slab, and the next, and the next.

"Help!" Stinko cries over the roaring wind. "It's got me!"

You watch helplessly as your little brother is towed away by an invisible force. Hot sand stings your eyes. You rub the grit away and focus on what is vacuuming up you and Stinko.

"It's the Sand Blob!" you scream to Stinko. "Fight it!"

The black hole in the Sand Blob is sucking in everything in its path. Slabs of slate fly over your head. Whole sand dunes whisk by you. Your skin burns as grains of sand sting you on their way into the black hole.

You wonder if you could tunnel down into the sand. You might escape from the Sand Blob that way.

Then you think: Or maybe . . .

Maybe the Sand Blob will take us out of here. Take us someplace better.

If you think the Sand Blob may be a way out of this awful desert, let it suck you over to PAGE 110.

If you quickly dig a hole to escape, turn to PAGE 90.

"What's happening?" Stinko cries.

"The tape!" you shout over the sounds of screaming cats. "The noise is making the whole place collapse! Run!"

But then a huge chunk of the concrete ceiling crashes down in front of you.

In front of the door.

You're trapped!

The wall of cages falls forward, crushing everything in the way. Zoe vanishes underneath the pile.

A large chunk of plaster peels away from a wall beside you. You peer through the hole. It opens directly to the outside.

Out of the Fun Zone!

"That way!" you shout.

You and Stinko lead the kids through the hole. Then you gather in a circle and watch the entire Fun Zone crumble.

"Wow!" says Stinko. "Wait until Mom hears about this!"

"Yeah," you agree. "Maybe next time she'll listen when I say I don't need a baby-sitter!"

THE END

"Rats!" you scream. "You want to turn us into rats?"

You struggle against the hands and claws that hold you.

"Don't let them!" Stinko wails.

"It will only be temporary," a creature with rat teeth, rat ears, and human eyes offers, tightening its grip on you.

"Being a rat isn't so bad," adds another mutant. "It's being half rat, half human that stinks."

"You only need to be rats long enough for us to collect some of your saliva," Zoe explains. "That's the missing ingredient in our secret formula. You must help us. You must!"

You gaze around. Some of the rat-people are switching back and forth between rat and human as fast as you switch your Game Boy on and off. With each change, they squeal in agony.

They must be miserable, you think.

"We'll switch you back," Zoe promises. "Trust us!"

The last time you trusted a bunch of rats, you ended up trapped in a tomb! Should you trust this group of half rats and eat the cheese?

Or does something tell you they don't call them rats for nothing?

If you and Stinko eat the cheese, go to PAGE 60.
If you refuse, go to PAGE 93.

"The dragon's breath is too hot!" you cry. "I have to let go! I have to cool down!"

You loosen your grip on the edge of the drawbridge. "Get ready to dive," you instruct Stinko. "Now!"

You let go and plunge toward the water.

Bad move! That's just what the hungry dragon was waiting for. He licks his dragon lips.

Then he exhales.

The burning blast of fire breath catches you and Stinko.

Instant barbecue!

You and Stinko are crispy critters now.

A little bit salty. But overall a tasty dragon treat!

THE END

You dig a hole and drag Stinko into it with you. You burrow down as deep as you can.

The Sand Blob roars over the hole. Brrr! That wind is not hot — it's freezing! You and Stinko huddle together.

Then — silence. The Blob is gone.

The hot ball of fire in the sky disappears.

A cool blue moon takes its place in a black sky.

You climb out of the hole and gaze around. The sand and the slate slabs have turned to ice! You take another step, and your ankles wobble. Your feet feel too heavy to lift.

"Ice skates!" Stinko exclaims behind you. "We're wearing ice skates! How did that happen?"

"I don't know," you admit. "But it's lucky we both know how to skate!"

You glide forward. Stinko follows you. Then he taps you. "You're it!" he yells, and skates away.

"Oh, no, you don't!" You laugh as you whiz by him. After all that terror, it feels good to kid around. "So long, Stinko!" you call back to him.

You skate right into Dare's tattooed arms!

Oops!

Go to PAGE 106.

You shut your eyes, bend your knees, and hurl yourself across the canyon.

Oh, no! You don't quite make it!

You slam stomach-first into the edge of the other side. Your fingers desperately claw at the dirt. It crumbles and falls around your head. Then you clasp a sturdy tree root.

Grunting, you pull yourself up over the edge. You lie flat on your back, panting. But you can't rest. The angry, evil baby-sitters scream and throw dirt bombs across the gorge.

You scramble to your feet. Perfect! Just ahead of you is a cave entrance. Above it a sign reads: TO THE BOTTOMLESS BALL PIT.

"So long, suckers!" you shout across to them. You've got to find Stinko and get out of this crazy place.

You duck into the cave. But instead of coming directly out the other side, you face a dark path — and another cave entrance.

Which do you take?

If you enter the cave within the cave, turn to PAGE 120.

If you stick to the path, turn to PAGE 76.

The elevator stops on the thirteenth floor. "This is where we get off," Dare announces harshly.

Using his only arm, he shoves you and Stinko out the door. A piece of a lizard tattoo falls off, leaving a new invisible spot on Dare's elbow.

"We're back in the tent where we started," you murmur to Stinko.

"But the tattoos on the walls aren't alive anymore," Stinko whispers back. You can hear the relief in his voice. "They're just pictures."

Dare pushes Stinko to the side. Then he shoves you to the center of the tent. You stumble a few steps.

"On the 'X'!" Dare orders you.

You notice two spotlights make a large 'X' on the floor.

You stand on it and wait.

Wait over on PAGE 75.

Trust these horrible creatures? Of course you don't!

"Forget it!" you yell. "No way!"

Nothing and no one can make you eat that yucky cheese. Not even these hideous mutants.

"That goes double for me!" Stinko hollers.

Zoe glares at you. "Wrong answer!"

The crowd of creatures drag you to the table beside Stinko. They strap you down.

"I think we should make examples of these two," the giant rat in the lab coat says ominously.

"Yes!" Zoe's rat whiskers twitch with excitement. "Let's force-feed them the Switch Cheese. And then let's do some experiments! Let them see how it feels to be lab animals!"

All the mutant rat-people let out horrible, shrill squeaks. You shudder. That must be mutant laughter! you realize.

Sorry. It looks as if you made a bad cheese — uh, choice. You thought you could end this adventure without eating any Switch Cheese. But that theory was full of holes!

Well, better hold your nose and get it over with. Because this is very definitely

THE END!

"Where's Dare?" Stinko whispers.

As usual, Dare is nowhere in sight. You sigh. "His favorite game must be hide-and-seek," you murmur.

"Right," Dare declares. Your eyes widen.

The tattooed man rises up from the tiles on the floor!

This guy is amazing! you admit to yourself. Scary — but amazing.

You peer at Dare. The spot where the spider tattoo used to be is empty. Dare has another invisible spot on his tattooed body.

Aha! Each time Dare loses a tattoo, you realize, he loses a piece of himself.

This fills you with courage. "What are you without your tattoos?" you demand. "Are you just a big nothing?"

Dare ignores your question. Instead, he swirls around. "Now you see me," Dare crows, waving his colorful cape. "Now you don't."

"Quit showing off, Dare!" you yell. "We want to go home!"

"To find your way home," Dare's voice taunts, "you'll have to find the way *out*!"

Go to PAGE 66.

You face the hideous monster, Dare. Is there any way out?

The elevator is still moving. There are no escape hatches.

Stinko whimpers behind you. Dare links his only arm through Stinko's arm and pulls your brother away from you.

"You can't hide from me. You've already taken too much of my time — and too much of me. I will win the game. I always win in the end."

"Let me go!" Stinko screams. He slaps at Dare's tattooed shoulder.

A shrunken Cyclops head in a hangman's noose comes off in Stinko's hand. Stinko screams and throws the hideous head to the floor. The one-eyed head rolls to a corner of the elevator and stops. It stares up at Dare.

"There's one last game to play," Dare hisses. "The most dangerous game of all. I call it 'All or Nothing.' You'll call it 'All *for* Nothing.' Are you ready to play?"

Well, are you?

If you're ready to play the most dangerous game, turn to PAGE 111.

If you stall and pick up the shrunken head, turn to PAGE 124.

"Come on, Stinko!" you exclaim. "Here's our chance!" You grab Stinko's hand and race to the fluttering edge of the tent.

Stinko gets down on his hands and knees and crawls out the opening. You follow right behind him.

Outside the tent, things are not what you expected. You thought you'd crawl to freedom — but you didn't think you'd be *this* free!

There's nothing above the tent.

There's nothing below the tent.

When you look back, even the tent is gone!

You've crawled out to the Edge of Nowhere! Will you drop off the edge?

Play the Edge of Nowhere game. The game will decide your fate! All you need are a coin and a tabletop. Place the coin at the table edge closest to you. Flick the coin to the other side of the table. Try to flick it as close to the edge as possible without letting it slide off the other side.

If you flick your coin over the edge, turn to PAGE 35.

If you flick your coin close to the edge but not over, turn to PAGE 78.

If you flick your coin and it doesn't come anywhere near the edge, try again. You don't want to be stuck on the Edge of Nowhere, do you?

You freeze, not daring to breathe. *Please don't find me*, you beg silently.

The shrill alarm grows louder. You glance toward the sound. At that moment there's a slight break in the drifting mist.

David! David is making that horrible screech!

And he's pointing straight at you!

He betrayed you!

Dozens of hippies swarm around David. "That way!" a skinny guy in a vest screams. "Don't let the kid get away!"

You clasp the railing and rush forward.

Oh, no! Zoe and the others are heading directly toward you. You glance back over your shoulder. The hippies are crowding onto the bridge. David is leading them right to you.

The bridge shakes under the weight of all the hippies piling onto it. It swings and sways. Mist swirls around you. Sometimes you see your pursuers, sometimes you don't.

Yikes! A hand grabs for you. You leap out of reach.

And right over the side of the bridge.

Oops! Klutzy move. You'll have to pay for that one. Yep. You're plummeting into a bottomless pit. You're falling and falling and falling —

And when you scream, "This is really the pits!" you mean it.

THE END

Dare steps toward you. All the tattoos seem to be spinning in your direction.

"Yikes!" you exclaim. You skate away from Dare and his evil army of living tattoos.

But you forgot you're only wearing one skate now. Instead of gliding, you trip over your blade.

The skate in your hand goes flying. The blade hits a hissing snake on Dare's ankle and sinks into the skin.

You watch in horror as the snake throws its slithering body forward. The skate blade digs in deeper.

Hissing and writhing, the snake tattoo falls from Dare's left ankle to the icy ground.

Right before your eyes, it disappears!

Go to PAGE 26.

Were you being questioned by an enormous cat?

Before you can ask, the creature vanishes. Light streams into the dim cave. You hear screams and squeals coming from just beyond the entrance.

You're not sure, but one of those squeals sounds a lot like Stinko's voice!

You stuff the tape into your pocket and run out of the cave.

Bingo! The cave opens onto a balcony overlooking the Bottomless Ball Pit. Zoe is nowhere in sight. You just might make it out of this place after all!

And there he is! Stinko! He's grinning broadly, preparing to dive into the ball pit.

You dash down the steps two at a time. You hurry to the edge of the pit. "Stinko!" you shout. But he can't hear you over all the cheers and squeals. He dives into the pool.

You rush to the edge.

But Stinko has vanished!

Go to PAGE 128.

"GAMES?" a deep voice behind you says. "If you want to play games, then I'm your guy!"

You and Stinko whirl around.

Zoe has vanished! In her place stands a tall, slim man wrapped in a long cape. His face, his body, and the cape are completely covered with tattoos! It's hard to tell where his body ends and his amazing cape begins!

"Where did you come from?" you demand.

"From Fun and Games KidsCare," the tattooed man explains. "Zoe's in charge of fun. I handle the games."

"Where's Zoe?" Stinko asks.

"Where the fun is," the man replies.

You can't tear your eyes away from the horrifying tattoos. Snakes slither up his arms. Dragons breathe flames across his chest. A Cyclops monster swings from a hangman's noose on one shoulder. Spiders, bats, and rats creep from his tattooed head to his tattooed feet.

The tattooed man swirls his cape. The tattoos dance wildly, making you dizzy. "They call me Dare," he tells you with a grin. "Ready to play games?"

Turn to PAGE 7.

"No!" you scream. "No! No! No!" You step out off the "X" and lunge forward.

Dare yanks back his Stinko arm and slams you on the side of the head.

The hit sends you reeling backwards. To stop yourself from falling, you grab the beast tattoo's horn.

To your shock, the horn pulls off in your hand. And with the horn comes the whole tattoo!

Once the beast has been torn from Dare's chest, the rest of the tattoos crumble.

Shrivel.

Dissolve.

"Aaaahhhhhhh!" Dare shrieks in agony. "You've destroyed me! I'm NOTHING! NOTHING! NOTHING!"

Yes! You did it! You beat Dare at his own game!

Go to PAGE 81.

"Not so fast!" Dare's voice repeats. "You're not out of the game yet!"

A grating noise makes your teeth ache. Then daylight suddenly streams into your eyes. You peer up. Dare stands over you, grinning. He's holding a wooden box top in his hands.

"What the . . . ?" you sputter, sitting up and rubbing your eyes. You gaze around.

Hey! You're not in a black hole at all.

You're inside the box that was in the middle of the tattooed tent! You recognize those tattooed walls.

You're back where you started!

Turn to PAGE 134.

Good work! You made it through the maze!

You emerge into a room full of huge tiled columns.

"I never thought we'd get out of there," Stinko admits. "How did you find the way?"

"It was easy," you tell him. "I just followed that rat." You point to a fat black rat scurrying away. "I figured he would know where he was going."

"Hey! I've seen that rat before," Stinko says.

"Where?" you ask.

Before he can answer you, one of the huge columns turns!

It's Dare!

"Here's where you've seen this rat before!" Dare announces. He holds out the palm of his left hand. The rat runs onto Dare's palm and settles into the skin.

It turns back into a rat tattoo!

"You bore me," Dare tells the rat. He peels it off of his palm, dangling it by its tail. It's a living rat again!

"I've got to hand it to you," Dare says. "You won my maze game." He blows on the twirling rodent. It disappears.

So does the palm of Dare's hand!

Turn to PAGE 40.

You give up. You blew it. You never should have trusted a kid with a furry claw instead of fingers!

"Eat the cheese!" David squeaks.

"Be one of us." Zoe pushes you to the ground and shoves the cheese under your nose. "Be all you can be."

Zoe presses the chunk of Switch Cheese against your mouth. You struggle, but Zoe just presses down harder. Dry crumbs stick to your lips. Your tongue darts out. You can't help it. You swallow.

Tingles shoot through your body. Fur sprouts from your skin. Your hands become claws. Your teeth sharpen.

The more you turn into a rat, the better the Switch Cheese tastes. When you've finished the hunk of cheese, Zoe pats your head and steps back.

You gaze up at her. She and David salute you.

Then a terrifying sight appears.

Stinko. Dressed in an army uniform.

It isn't his rat face, his long twitchy tail, or his wiggling whiskers that fill you with disgust and horror.

No, it's the unbelievable, terrifying reality that in the rat-people's army — your kid brother out-ranks you!

THE END

You try to look at Dare, but his body is too horrifying. Instead, you lock onto his eyes.

Weird, you think. His eyes don't match. One is green, but the other is blue.

You feel dizzy. His eyes seem to spin. The word ALL appears in his green eye. In the blue eye you see the word NOTHING.

Now you know.

The choice is in his eyes!

Your mind spins too. Questions swirl around in your head. Is this a trap? Why does the choice seem so obvious?

If you take ALL, will you win all?

If you take NOTHING, will you win nothing?

What could this monster, Dare, have up his remaining sleeve?

Use the Spinner on PAGE 136 to help you make the ALL or NOTHING choice. Follow the directions at the top of the page.

If your finger lands on ALL, go to PAGE 54.

If your finger lands on NOTHING, go to PAGE 122.

"Let me go!" you scream. You wrestle to break Dare's grip on your arm. But he clutches you tightly.

"Welcome back," Dare says.

Stinko skates by. Dare snags him too. "You've made it to another level," he remarks. "Time for the next game. And this game is very cool. Freezing, in fact!"

Dare reaches under his cape and pulls out a silver spray gun. On the barrel it says: INSTANT ICE MAKER.

Before you can protest, he takes aim and sprays Stinko. Stinko instantly freezes.

He's an ice statue!

"Stinko!" you cry.

Dare turns the ice gun on you.

Turn to PAGE 28.

You're not going to risk running smack into Zoe. You glance around, searching for another way back to Stinko.

You spot a path at the edge of the canyon. Maybe it will lead you back to the cave entrance. You scuffle through the thick vegetation and start following the path.

"Eeeeeeee!" A shrill, shrieking alarm stops you in your tracks. You peer through the mist and trees.

David! He's making that awful sound! His face twists in a nasty grimace.

His teeth. They're *fangs*!

"Eeeeeeeeee!" he trills again.

You knew you couldn't trust him! You start to run.

"The kid!" you hear Zoe cry. "Over there!"

Roots grab at your feet. Leaves smack your face. You glance back.

Oh, no! Zoe has been joined by dozens of pointy-nosed hippies. They're right behind you!

If you stay on the path, they will catch you for sure. You stare at the canyon. It's much narrower here. It might be ten feet across, maybe less. Maybe more.

Can you jump across?

There's no time for choices now. Just do it. Leap to PAGE 91.

The Dare ice melts first.

"Aha!" Dare cheers. "I win the Cool Contest. And that was just a warm-up!"

What now? you wonder.

Dare turns his back to you and spreads his cape open like butterfly wings. A fire-breathing dragon tattoo on the cape spits out a blowtorch blast of flames. The thick coat of ice on you and Stinko melts instantly.

Oh, no! The ice beneath your feet also thaws. You and Stinko are suddenly neck deep in freezing, swirling water!

You dog-paddle furiously. You strain to keep your head above the water.

A large stone castle looms over you. You realize you're in a moat circling the castle. Your gaze rises up . . . and up.

It lands on Dare, high in a turret.

"Look at that!" Stinko whimpers behind you.

You turn in the cold water.

Whoa! A giant dragon hovers at the edge of the ice. You recognize it as the dragon tattoo from Dare's cape!

Somehow, it slid off the cape and into real life!

And it's getting ready to blast you again!

Go to PAGE 51.

Your stomach lurches as you gape at the bizarre creatures. Some have human bodies with rat heads. Some have rat bodies and human faces. Others are a disgusting mix of both!

Two gigantic all-rat rats stand at the head of the table. They wear lab coats that fit awkwardly over their huge, furry bodies. Their whiskers twitch as they shove their pointy faces at Stinko.

"Leave me alone," Stinko whimpers.

The little stinker may drive you crazy, but you can't let those monster mutants hurt him.

You jump down, landing with a soft thud. "What are you doing to Stinko?" you demand. You lunge through the crowd of rats.

Instantly, dozens of hands and claws clutch you. You're caught!

You can't escape, so flip to PAGE 8.

You decide to let the Sand Blob suck you up. Wherever you end up has got to be better than this awful desert!

You stop resisting. You and Stinko fly forward with the raging sand and wind.

"The Sand Blob is swallowing us!" Stinko shrieks.

You're sucked into the Sand Blob. The roaring stops. The black hole closes behind you. You are in total darkness now.

"It's squashing me!" Stinko moans.

You know exactly what he means. The blackness presses in all around you. You can practically feel it. It's like walls, pushing you down . . . flattening you. . . .

"I'm sorry," you tell Stinko. "I guess we lose this time. The Sand Blob got us in

THE

"Not so fast!" a familiar deep voice calls out. "Turn to PAGE 102!"

You heard him! Turn to PAGE 102!

You swallow hard. "All right," you declare. "I'm ready. All or nothing!"

Dare is a sickening sight to see. His tattooed cape is gone. His tattooed form shrivels as each tattoo wears itself out trying to hold Dare together.

Many of Dare's dangers are gone. The dragon, the snake, the rat, the cyclone, and now even the shrunken Cyclops head have all been peeled away.

What could be worse than all of those things you've already destroyed?

Don't worry. Dare is about to show you.

Go to PAGE 92.

112

Zoe must have guessed what you're thinking. "Don't worry," she assures you. "All you have to do to return to normal is eat a little more Switch Cheese."

Zoe holds the Switch Cheese in front of you and Stinko. You each gobble up the cheese. Instantly the change takes place.

You wiggle your human fingers. Whew. That's a relief!

"That was fun!" Stinko cries. "Let's do it again!"

The rat leader returns, hovering in the doorway. "The new formula is complete!" he announces.

"Yay!" Zoe cheers.

The remaining rat-people in the lab race through the doorway. The door shuts with a loud bang.

"Wait!" you call after them. "You forgot to tell us how to get home!"

No answer.

The mutants are gone.

You flop down on a table. "Great!" you groan. "We help them — and they leave us here with no way to get back home!"

Flip to PAGE 85.

You gulp in some air and force your way through the bobbing balls. You push your arms forward in a breaststroke and kick your feet. Balls pop up into the air around you.

But finally you reach your little brother.

"Stinko!" you call to him.

He turns at the sound of your voice. His face is twisted into a look of terror. For once he doesn't try to get away from you.

"Help me!" he cries. He reaches for your outstretched hand.

As soon as Stinko grabs your hand, you both sink down through the balls. "Whoa!" you exclaim.

Then you notice other kids are sinking too.

Something on the bottom of this pit is sucking you in!

You peer down. There's a giant Plexiglas tube at the bottom of the ball pit. It's like a drain!

There's no stopping the suction now. You're spiraling downward — and taking Stinko with you.

You take one last desperate gulp of air as you are pulled through the tube.

Come out on PAGE 44.

114

There's no way you're going to send Stinko on such an important mission. Those keys are your only hope for escape. This is no job for a little brother.

You suck in your stomach and start squirming through the bent bars.

"Where are you going?" Stinko whimpers. "Don't leave me."

"Don't worry," you say. "I can't. I'm stuck!"

It's true. Even with your stomach sucked way in, the narrow space between the bars has you trapped.

And you can hear the rat people returning!

"Well, well!" Zoe cheers as she re-enters the room. "I see we have a volunteer!"

Is she talking to you?

Uh-oh . . .

Turn to PAGE 133.

Join the rat-people's army?

"No way!" you shout.

You knock the chunk of Switch Cheese out of Zoe's claw. It falls to the ground.

You turn to run, but David throws himself down on the ground in front of you. You trip over him and fall flat on your face.

You scramble to your feet. But before you can run, David grabs the back of your shirt. And then wraps his stringy rat tail around your right ankle, holding you fast!

"Nice work," Zoe compliments the rat-boy. She tosses him another bite of cheese as a reward. His nose twitches as he chews it gratefully.

"Time to eat your Switch Cheese." Zoe's glittering rat eyes gaze at you. "And this time you won't get away from me!"

Give up. Just go to PAGE 104.

116

Yes! You have the tape! Now what was it the voice in the dark said when you asked what was on the tape?

"You will find out when it becomes necessary."

Hmm. Could the voice have meant now?

You pull the tape from your pocket and pop it into the boom box. You cross your fingers for luck. Then you push PLAY.

Instantly, ear-splitting cat screeches blast through the room. Howls and wails bounce off the walls.

The mutant rats are terrified! They don't realize the awful sounds are coming from the tape.

They believe there are dozens of cats in the room!

Hurrying to escape the cats, the mutant rats go berserk. They dive under the counters, climb up the tables, and scurry behind anything that will hide them.

This is your chance to grab the keys and release the other kids. You unlock all the cages.

"This way!" you call. The kids scramble to follow you out the door.

With the cat tape shrieking, the rats scurrying, and the kids running, the whole room starts to shake!

"Hurry!" you cry. "Before it's too late!"

Run to PAGE 87.

Whoops! You picked the string that's sure to leave you at loose ends.

You find yourself all alone outside the parachute.

Dangling from the string. In midair!

Stinko and Dare have vanished.

There is nothing above or below you. Cold air blows through you. Darkness folds in around you as you swing back and forth.

Can you *please* try to be more careful next time? Because nobody likes to be left hanging!

THE END

118

"Up!" you shout. You pull your brother inside and pound the DOOR CLOSE button. "Close! Close! Close!" you mutter.

Zoe reaches the elevator just as the doors slide shut. You shiver at the sight of the rat-faced babysitter. It's twisted into an expression of fury.

"No!" you hear Zoe snarl. "They can't get away!"

The elevator motor starts. You and Stinko slide to the floor, huffing and puffing. You lean back against the wall. "We made it," you breathe.

This is the first chance you've had to rest for even a second. You shut your eyes. Stinko leans his head against your shoulder. You're almost feeling relaxed, when you hear a tapping noise above you.

You glance up and see a giant rat's claw.

Breaking through the ceiling!

Go to PAGE 48.

You gasp at the sight of the clawed hand. But you're not going to let your fear keep you from being rescued!

"Thanks for saving me," you tell the boy as he pulls you to safety. You peer at him. He looks a little older than Stinko, but younger than you.

"I'm David." He holds out his hairy hand to shake. But when he sees you staring at it, he shoves it into his pocket.

"Wh-wh-what happened to you?" you stammer.

"I don't know," David admits. "It started as soon as the KidScare baby-sitter went to check in at the gate."

"Hey! We came with a sitter from the same agency!" you cry.

"There's something really weird going on here," David warns you. "The baby-sitters are evil."

"Evil?" Your voice trembles. "What do you —"

"Sshhh!" David interrupts you. "Listen!"

You hear voices approaching. One is Zoe's.

"We can't let them find us!" David gasps. "Follow me!"

You're not sure if you trust this kid. That hairy hand of his gives you the creeps.

But so does Zoe! And she's getting closer.

If you decide to trust this strange boy, go to PAGE 125.

If you'd rather go your own way, turn to PAGE 55.

120

You remember that there were cave entrances near the ball pit. You step into the cave, hoping that's where it leads. You blink your eyes, trying to focus in the pitch darkness.

"Who enters my cave?" a deep voice booms.

Fear clutches your throat. What have you gotten yourself into now?

"Uh — it's just me," you croak.

"Why have you trespassed?" the voice demands.

"I'm running from a pack of evil baby-sitters," you blurt.

Oops! You hope you're not talking to one of them!

"Those baby-sitters are the worst!" the voice growls.

Whew!

"So you'll let me through?" you ask nervously.

You wish you could see who you're talking to. You strain your eyes. But it's just too dark.

"Not so fast," the voice snaps. "First, you must answer three questions. If you pass my test, I'll let you pass *me*."

Turn to PAGE 31.

"I choose green!" you declare.

Uh-oh. Maybe that wasn't the right choice. Dare laughs so hard, his tattoos shake, rattle, and roll all over his body.

"Green?" he chokes out. "You choose green? Don't you know what it means to choose green?"

"Hey!" Stinko exclaims, peering at you. "You're a frog! A green frog!"

At least, that's what he tries to say. Actually, what comes out sounds more like, "Ribbit! Ribbit! Ribbit ribbiiiit!"

But you understand him perfectly. Because all frogs speak the same language.

"Ribbit ribbit, ribbit," you reply. "Ribbit."

Which means, "You're a frog too, Stinko."

Oh, well. You jump — but not for joy at the way this adventure has come to the

RIBBIT!

(Which, you probably know, means END in froggy talk.)

"I choose NOTHING!" you exclaim.

The horned beast on Dare's chest roars. It reaches for you with a clawed hand.

"Stop!" Stinko shouts. He runs to your side.

"Get back!" Dare bellows. "This game is just between us!"

Stinko clutches your leg. "I won't leave you," he cries.

The beast on Dare's chest reaches for Stinko!

You try to hang on to him, but the beast is too strong. It drags your little brother into its arms. Then the killer beast tattoo slams Stinko against Dare's shoulder.

A new tattoo instantly appears. And a whole new arm.

"No!" you shriek. You shut your eyes. You can't look at the horrible sight.

Stinko is the tattoo creating this new arm!

Dare's laughter sounds like a cry of victory. "You chose NOTHING," he shouts. "And NOTHING is what you will get! No points, no brother, no home, no life, no NOTHING!"

You can't believe your choice is turning out so badly. Stinko is a tattoo! You know you'll be next.

You can't let the game end this way.

Can you?

Go to PAGE 101.

You take another step onto the rope bridge. You force yourself to stay calm as it swings wildly. Clutching the railing tightly, you tiptoe across the ropes.

You can hear Zoe and the other baby-sitters talking in the middle of the orange mist. "That kid won't get away from us," Zoe snarls. "They never escape for long."

You hug the rope railing and pull yourself blindly into the thick mist. You know you're very close to them, but so far they haven't sensed you.

You just might make it!

Then a loud, shrill shriek pierces the mist.

"That's the kid alarm!" Zoe cries. "Get the kid!"

Hold your breath until PAGE 97.

124

You grab the shrunken Cyclops head by its stringy black hair. You swing it around like a lasso. Dare ducks to avoid being hit.

Oops! The one-eyed monster clobbers you on its way around.

You drop the head and collapse. You're knocked out cold.

You don't know how much time has passed. You hear Stinko's voice next to you. "Wake up!" he's saying.

You open one eye. You're back in your own room!

In your own house!

"Wake up!" Stinko yells, shaking your shoulder. "They're back!"

You squint your eyes to see the couple standing in the doorway of your room. "Mom? Dad?" you ask groggily.

"Ready for some fun?" one of them asks.

"And some games?" demands the other.

Oh, no! It's not your mom and dad.

It's Zoe and Dare.

Zoe grins at you. A nasty, ratlike grin. "Your mom called. They're staying an extra week. So — ready for fun and games?"

"This isn't fun at all!" you wail.

"Then it must be games," Dare declares.

Go to PAGE 7.

He may be weird-looking, but you trust David. Besides, how much choice do you have?

"Okay," you agree. "Which way?"

"Follow me," he whispers. He holds out his claw.

Taking a deep breath, you grasp his furry hand. Shivers race along your neck. But by holding hands and clutching the side rails, the two of you are able to keep your balance.

"Made it!" you cheer, stepping onto solid ground.

David glances over his shoulder. "Hurry. We don't have much time! The baby-sitters are headed this way."

This side of the canyon doesn't look like a forest at all. Instead of lush plants and bushes, you seem to be in a large gymnasium. The towering trees lining the edge of the canyon hid the setup completely, you realize.

"Owww!" You tumble over with a thud. You were so busy gazing around that you never noticed — you walked right into two rows of tires lying on the ground.

David yanks you upright. "Watch where you're going."

Lifting your knees high, you dash through the tires. Then you and David come to a towering wall. Ropes dangle from the top of it.

"We've got to climb over that?" you gasp.

Go to PAGE 12.

126

You grit your teeth and pull yourself up, up, up. Stinko hangs on to your ankles.

Finally you flop onto the drawbridge, dragging Stinko behind you. The dragon shoots out one last fiery blast.

It misses you.

As the drawbridge goes up, you and Stinko slide down and tumble into the castle. You land on a colorful mosaic-tile floor. The bridge bangs closed. A heavy iron bar locks it in place.

You and Stinko survived the moat. And the dragon.

But now you're trapped inside the castle.

"Welcome to KidScare Castle," Dare's voice bellows all around you. "Congratulations! You've made it this far! Not many others have survived the games. You may get home yet."

As he speaks, you glimpse something moving near your foot.

You peer down.

Yuck!

A huge, hairy, red-eyed spider crawls across your sneaker. You recognize it! It's the spider tattoo from Dare's left hand.

He lost another tattoo!

Go to PAGE 94.

"Aaaaaaahhhhh!" With a howl, you dart across the cluttered basement. Dashing through a doorway, you find yourself in another dim corridor. You have no idea where it leads, but it doesn't matter. The rats are chasing you.

They're less than a whisker's length behind you!

You tear along the hallway. You spot three doors up ahead. Maybe, just maybe, you can reach one of the doors — and save yourself from the rats!

The rats squeak and snap at your heels. Your breath comes in gasps. Hurry! Hurry! you urge yourself silently.

You approach the doors. The rats swarm around you. They make it impossible for you to go through any door but the one in the middle.

A weird thought crosses your mind. Do the rats actually *want* you to choose that door?

No way, you tell yourself. Impossible!

You yank open the middle door and slam it shut behind you.

"Whew!" you breathe. You lean against the door. "Safe!"

Are you sure?

Find out on PAGE 4.

"Stinko!" you yell as loud as you can.

It's no use wasting your breath. He can't hear you. He has sunk from view. Buried in colored plastic balls.

You've got to get him out of there. And then you've got to get both of you out of the Fun Zone.

But how?

You notice heavy ropes dangling over the pit. If you could just grab one of the ropes, you might be able to swing over the pit and yank Stinko out.

That is, if he comes up to the surface, you remind yourself.

You could dive in. But it would be very hard to find him among all those kids and plastic balls.

You know Zoe is going to show up any minute. And Stinko is definitely not going to come out of the ball pit on his own.

What should you do?

If you jump in, turn to PAGE 42.
If you go for the rope, go to PAGE 68.

What's that? You don't have the cassette tape? Too bad.

Listen up. We're about to tell you something important:

Next time you read this story, make sure you go through the caves!

Meanwhile, it's time to pay for your mistake.

Pay up on PAGE 133.

"Zoe!" you repeat as the mutant rat-girl completes her transformation. "What — ? How — ? But — "

"I'm one of them," she explains. "I was sent among the humans to bring you and Stinko here. You will help us fix the laboratory mistake."

"We will?" Your voice trembles.

What could these horrible creatures want with you and your little brother?

Before you can ask, Zoe shrieks in agony.

Turn to PAGE 74.

"Noooooo," you moan in horror. Stinko whimpers beside you. He grabs your hand.

He must be really afraid!

You can't tear your eyes away from the awful sight. The more you stare, the more you think you recognize the creature.

Unbelievable, but . . . it looks like Zoe!

But if it is Zoe, she is trapped somewhere between human and rat. Like an experiment gone horribly wrong.

Her head is shaped like a rat's, but her eyes and lips are human. Her fur is as long as human hair. It covers a rat body with human legs and arms.

Her hands are gnarled masses of fingers and claws. Yellow rat teeth poke, knifelike, out of her human mouth.

Then you see something even worse.

Yes, worse than a giant, mutant rat-person.

Dozens of giant, mutant rat-people.

Coming straight toward you!

Go to PAGE 11.

"No!" you shriek. You're too terrified to move.

The rats crawl all over you. Their claws scrape your skin. Their teeth graze your flesh.

You shut your eyes tightly. Your heart pounds with revulsion and fear. Are the rats going to eat you alive?

Then you realize:

The rats aren't eating *you*.

They're eating the *worms* that still cling to your clothes.

But when they finish off the worms, will you be next?

Your science teacher told you that rats are smart and don't deserve the bad rap they get. But you don't care. They are too gross!

You've got to get out of here! But how? Even if you get out from under the rats, you'll still have to escape them.

Jump up, shake them off, and run away on PAGE 127.

Remove them slowly and gently on PAGE 6.

"You can go first," Zoe tells you with a nasty grin.

She and the other mutants swarm around your cage. They yank you out and drag you into the laboratory.

"Start the Kid Grater!" Zoe orders.

It only takes a few seconds for Zoe and the others to place you in the mechanical arm of the giant Kid Grater. The process is so fast you hardly know what's happening.

All you know is, when it comes to secret ingredients, you are the GRATE-est!

THE END

"You're sitting on me," Stinko complains, shoving you with his elbow. "What's going on? Let me out!"

He scrambles over the side of the box. You follow him.

The moment you stand up, you wish you hadn't.

You feel woozy. The moving tattoos on the tent walls are making your head ache.

"I'm going to give you a second chance," Dare tells you.

Then he swirls his tattooed cape around his body — and melts into the walls!

Where did he go? you wonder. You rub your eyes and try to steady yourself. Everything feels familiar. It's as if you've done this all before.

But you can't remember where. Or when.

In fact, the harder you try, the less you can remember!

Gazing around, you spot an opening in the wall of the tent.

Hmm. Maybe you should try to get out of this place.

Or have you already done that?

You aren't sure. But something tells you you should get moving.

Go back to PAGE 96. And take a hint: Next time you meet the Sand Blob, don't let it suck you up!

"Hello, this message is for Zoe," the recording begins.

You gasp. You know that voice.

It's your mom!

Your heart pounds hard as you listen to Mom's message:

"We got your message letting us know everything is fine. Thanks for taking such good care of the kids! We're so glad we left them with you. And we're glad you can stay longer, because we've decided to extend our trip for another week!"

You and Stinko stare at each other in pure horror.

Another week? Another week of Dare's horrible games?

"No! I can't take it!" you wail, sinking to the floor.

Oh, well. What can you do? Guess you'll have to grin and Dare it!

THE END

136

FUN AND GAMES SPINNER

This is your Official Spinner. Guard it with your life! This Spinner will help you make important choices throughout the *Attack of the Beastly Baby-sitter*. Follow these simple finger-spinning instructions each time you use the Spinner.

Finger-Spinning Instructions: There are four Choice Rings in this Spinner. Place your index finger on the correct Choice Ring. Close your eyes (no peeking!). Circle your finger around and around and around (keep circling!) until you feel like stopping. Open your eyes. Read the word under your finger. Your choice has been made for you!

About R.L. Stine

R.L. STINE is the most popular author in America. He is the creator of the *Goosebumps*, *Give Yourself Goosebumps*, *Fear Street*, and *Ghosts of Fear Street* series, among other popular books. He has written more than 100 scary novels for kids. Bob lives in New York City with his wife, Jane, teenage son, Matt, and dog, Nadine.

GOT Goosebumps YET?

by R.L. Stine

GOOSEBUMPS

GOOSEBUMPS PRESENTS

☐ BAB93954-8	TV Episode #7: The Headless Ghost	$3.99
☐ BAB93955-6	TV Episode #8: Be Careful What You Wish For	$3.99
☐ BAB93959-9	TV Episode #9: Go Eat Worms!	$3.99
☐ BAB62836-4	Tales to Give You Goosebumps Book & Light Set Special Edition #1	$11.95
☐ BAB26603-9	More Tales to Give You Goosebumps Book & Light Set Special Edition #2	$11.95
☐ BAB74150-4	Even More Tales to Give You Goosebumps Book and Boxer Shorts Pack Special Edition #3	$14.99

———— GIVE YOURSELF GOOSEBUMPS ————

☐ BAB55323-2	#1: Escape from the Carnival of Horrors	$3.99
☐ BAB56645-8	#2: Tick Tock, You're Dead	$3.99
☐ BAB56646-6	#3: Trapped in Bat Wing Hall	$3.99
☐ BAB67318-1	#4: The Deadly Experiments of Dr. Eeek	$3.99
☐ BAB67319-X	#5: Night in Werewolf Woods	$3.99
☐ BAB67320-3	#6: Beware of the Purple Peanut Butter	$3.99
☐ BAB67321-1	#7: Under the Magician's Spell	$3.99
☐ BAB84765-1	#8: The Curse of the Creeping Coffin	$3.99
☐ BAB84766-X	#9: The Knight in Screaming Armor	$3.99
☐ BAB84767-8	#10: Diary of a Mad Mummy	$3.99
☐ BAB84768-6	#11: Deep in the Jungle of Doom	$3.99
☐ BAB84772-4	#12: Welcome to the Wicked Wax Museum	$3.99
☐ BAB84773-2	#13: Scream of the Evil Genie	$3.99
☐ BAB84774-0	#14: The Creepy Creations of Professor Shock	$3.99

☐ BAB53770-9	The Goosebumps Monster Blood Pack	$11.95
☐ BAB50995-0	The Goosebumps Monster Edition #1	$12.95
☐ BAB93371-X	The Goosebumps Monster Edition #2	$12.95
☐ BAB60265-9	Goosebumps Official Collector's Caps Collecting Kit	$5.99
☐ BAB73906-9	Goosebumps Postcard Book	$7.95
☐ BAB73902-6	The 1997 Goosebumps 365 Scare-a-Day Calendar	$8.95
☐ BAB73907-7	The Goosebumps 1997 Wall Calendar	$10.99

Scare me, thrill me, mail me GOOSEBUMPS now!

Available wherever you buy books, or use this order form. Scholastic Inc., P.O. Box 7502,
2931 East McCarty Street, Jefferson City, MO 65102

Please send me the books I have checked above. I am enclosing $ _____ (please add $2.00 to cover shipping and handling). Send check or money order — no cash or C.O.D.s please.

Name _____ Age _____

Address _____

City _____ State/Zip _____

Please allow four to six weeks for delivery. Offer good in the U.S. only. Sorry, mail orders are not available to residents of Canada. Prices subject to change.